UNCANNY
ENCOUNTERS:
ROSWELL

Jean Rabe
Nick Redfern
Stephen D. Sullivan
Robert E. Vardeman
& Jim Holloway

Walkabout Publishing • 2008

Walkabout Publishing
S.D.Studios
P.O.Box 151
Kansasville, WI 53139
www.walkaboutpublishing.com

ISBN: 978-0-9802086-9-6

For our many uncanny friends and fans.

CONTENTS

INTRODUCTION

A "Cosmic Watergate" UFO researcher Stanton Friedman calls what happened at Roswell—a cover-up of the first known contact between the human race and alien beings.

"A Project Mogul balloon," the military insists. No flying saucer, no alien bodies, no unfathomable wreckage—just a secret military project covered up during the Cold War. After that, rumor became legend, and people's memories started playing tricks.

That's the story, anyway.

Which version of Roswell is true? Ask any two people and you'll probably get different answers from both. UFO researchers side with Friedman; skeptics with the military. For most of us, it's hard to tell where Roswell's reality ends and its myth begins.

In *Uncanny Encounters: Roswell*, our authors give you both. You'll get the facts and the mythology from paranormal researcher supreme, Nick Redfern. You also get three speculative (or if you prefer "fictional") takes on the events, supplied by authors Robert E. Vardeman, Jean Rabe, and Stephen D. Sullivan—storytellers with over 150 published books between them. Plus, you get a really nifty cover by renowned fantasy and Sci-Fi illustrator, Jim Holloway.

Hopefully, this book will both enlighten and amuse you.

After reading, you can make up your own mind where the truth actually lies. (And be sure to look for future books in the *Uncanny Encounters*™ series!)

Enjoy.

— Steve Sullivan
Walkabout Publishing Founder
December, 2008

ROSWELL
Part I: The Crash
by Nick Redfern

"RAAF Captures Flying Saucer on Ranch in Roswell Region," was the headline that leapt from the front page of the 8 July 1947 edition of the *Roswell Daily Record*, a newspaper named after the small New Mexican town whose people it served. Amazingly, this was not some fanciful story concocted by an enterprising hoaxer. Rather, the newspaper caption was based upon the following, officially sanctioned, press release issued by Walter Haut, the Press Information Officer at the nearby Roswell Army Air Field:

"The many rumors regarding the flying disc became a reality yesterday when the Intelligence office of the 509th Bomb Group of the Eighth Air Force, Roswell Army Air Field, was fortunate to gain possession of a disc through the cooperation of one of the local ranchers and the sheriff's office of Chaves County.

"The flying object landed on a ranch near Roswell sometime last week. Not having phone facilities, the rancher stored the disc until such time as he was able to contact the sheriff's office, who in turn notified Maj. Jesse A. Marcel of the 509th Bomb Group Intelligence Office.

"Action was immediately taken and the disc was picked up at the rancher's home. It was inspected at the Roswell Army Air Field and subsequently loaned by Major Marcel to higher headquarters." (1)

Shortly after this astonishing news had spread quite literally around the world, another announcement was made: the whole thing had been a false alarm. What had in fact been recovered was merely the radar reflector from an errant weather balloon. To bolster this explanation, Brigadier General Roger Ramey, of the Eighth Air Force at Fort Worth, Texas, allowed press photographers to take shots of the debris from a stricken balloon, which had been laid out on the floor of a small office at the base.

Despite the decidedly unimpressive-looking nature of the wreckage on display for the photographers, the media apparently chose not to express its incredulity that anyone could confuse what was obviously weather balloon-borne debris with something potentially more exotic. The official explanation was accepted and, at a stroke, interest in the story dwindled and the entire matter was laid to rest. That situation remained practically unchanged for thirty years.

Stanton T. Friedman obtained his Masters of Science in Physics at the University of Chicago in 1956 and, for the next fourteen years, worked as a nuclear physicist for a variety of organizations, including General Electric, Aerojet General, Westinghouse, and General Motors. During that time Friedman developed an intense interest in UFOs and, in 1970, began to lecture on the subject on a full-time basis. **(2)**

On 20 January 1978, Friedman was in Baton Rouge, Louisiana, to give a lecture at the State University, and while in the city he agreed to take part in a number of media interviews that had been arranged by an associate. One such interview took place at a local television station. During a break Friedman was introduced to the station manager, who, as luck would have it, was a friend of the by-then-retired Jesse Marcel and basic details of the Roswell affair were imparted to Friedman. Acting on this information, he wasted no time in contacting Marcel, who had a most interesting story to tell concerning what happened back in 1947. **(3)**

"I saw a lot of wreckage but no complete machine," said Marcel, explaining that whatever the object was, it must have exploded in the air. "It had disintegrated before it hit the ground. The wreckage was scattered over an area about three quarters of a mile long and several hundred feet wide.

"I was pretty well acquainted with most everything that was in the air at that time, both ours and foreign," Marcel continued. "I was also acquainted with virtually every type of weather-observation or radar-tracking device being used by either the civilians or the military."

Marcel added that in his opinion the debris was not from a weather-tracking device, nor was it from an aircraft or a missile. "What it was we didn't know. We just picked up the fragments." Marcel was certain, however, that the debris was unlike anything he had ever seen before or since, and that "it certainly wasn't anything built by us." (4)

During the course of his investigations Friedman hooked up with William Moore, a writer and researcher who expressed an interest in pursuing the case further and who had his own leads that seemed to have a positive bearing on the Marcel account. As a result of their inquiries, Friedman and Moore were able to confirm where the unusual debris had been found: the Foster Ranch, a remote piece of land located in an area some seventy-five miles north of the town of Roswell, New Mexico, and worked by one William Ware "Mac" Brazel. Regrettably, Brazel had long since passed away; however, his friends and family, some of whom still lived in the vicinity, recalled the incident well.

Commenting on the strange material found on the ranch, Brazel's son, Bill, stated that it was: "...something on the order of tinfoil except that [it] wouldn't tear...You could wrinkle it and lay it back down and it immediately resumed its original shape. [It was] quite pliable, but you couldn't crease or bend it like ordinary metal. Almost like a plastic, but definitely metallic in nature. Dad once said that the Army had once told him it was not anything made by us." (5)

Jesse Marcel also elaborated on the extraordinary properties present in the material that he recovered: "[It] could not be bent or broken...or even dented by a sixteen-pound sledge hammer. Almost weightless...like a metal with plastic properties." (6)

A further lead came from Vern and Jean Maltais, who stated that a friend of theirs, Grady Barnett, a field engineer with the Soil Conservation Service, had confided in them that he had come across a grounded object ("a kind of disk [that] looked like dirty stainless steel") in the New Mexico desert in the vicinity of the Plains of San Agustin, around which were a number of small, and quite dead, bodies of an unusual nature. All were small in stature, with large, pear-shaped heads, "oddly spaced eyes," skinny arms and legs and completely hairless. Needless to say, the military quickly arrived on the scene and assumed control of the situation. (7)

As the 1970s drew to a close, enough data had been gathered to warrant the publication of a full-length book on the case: *The Roswell Incident*, co-authored by Moore and the late writer Charles Berlitz, was published in 1980. (8) By 1985, research had uncovered almost a hundred people who had been implicated in the events at Roswell in some capacity. The official "weather balloon" explanation was crumbling fast.

In July 1985, Moore gave a presentation at the annual symposium of the Mutual UFO Network (MUFON) at St. Louis, Missouri. During the course of his lecture, Moore revealed what had occurred when Friedman brought up the matter of the unusual bodies with Lewis "Bill" Rickett, a former Counter Intelligence Corps (CIC) officer stationed at Roswell at the time of the incident. The following is Friedman's own assessment of the interview: "When I mentioned bodies, Rickett clearly reacted and indicated that this was an area he couldn't talk about. He indicated there were different levels of security about this work - that a directive had come down placing this at a high level. He went on to say that certain subjects were discussed only in rooms that couldn't be bugged." (9)

Notably, Rickett has been identified as one of at least two men (the other being Rickett's superior with the CIC, Sheridan

Ware Cavitt, about who more later) who accompanied Major Marcel back to the Foster Ranch to inspect the mysterious debris.

In addition to the research of Moore and Friedman, further information surfaced in the late 1980s and 1990s from the investigative team of Kevin Randle and Don Schmitt. Randle, a captain in the Air Force Reserve, and Schmitt co-wrote two books on the Roswell controversy suggesting that on the night of 4 July 1947, an extra-terrestrial spacecraft crashed to earth some miles from the town of Roswell having already deposited a sizeable amount of debris on the Foster Ranch. In contrast to the accepted wisdom, the vehicle, asserted several of the pair's sources, was rather narrow with a bat-like wing and no longer than thirty feet in length – this point having been stressed particularly by CIC man Lewis Rickett. **(10)** Similarly, Thomas Gonzalez, who was stationed at Roswell Army Air Field on returning to the States after the end of the Second World War, described the vehicle as an "airfoil;" Johnny McBoyle, reporter and part-owner of KSWS radio station in Roswell, recalled seeing a "big crumpled dishpan;" and Frank Kauffman referred to the object as being "heel-shaped." **(11)**

Interestingly, according to Lewis Rickett, in September 1947 he became embroiled in the Roswell affair at a deep level when he spent a period of time working with a Dr. Lincoln La Paz of the University of New Mexico. Lincoln La Paz was born in Wichita, Kansas in 1897 and, having enrolled at the University of Chicago, obtained a Ph.D. in 1928 and wrote his thesis on the calculus of variations under the direction of Gilbert Ames Bliss. After a brief stint as National Research Fellow and as instructor at Chicago, La Paz was hired as assistant professor at Ohio State in 1930 and was promoted to associate professor in 1936 and then to professor in 1942. While at Ohio State, La Paz was very active in developing the graduate program in mathematics, directing three Ph.D. students, including Earl J. Mickle.

During the Second World War, while on leave from Ohio State, he served as Research Mathematician at the New Mexico Proving Ground and as Technical Director, Operations Analysis Section, with the Second Air Force. During this period his interests shifted to ballistics and then, specifically to the study of meteorites.

In 1945, La Paz joined the faculty of the University of New Mexico and founded the Institute of Meteoritics, where he remained as director until 1966. From 1945 to 1953 he also served as Head of the Department of Mathematics and Astronomy and, from 1953 to 1962, as Director of the Division of Astronomy.

La Paz was a pioneer in the field of meteoritics. At a time when meteorites were widely viewed as curiosities, he had the vision to recognize their scientific significance and established active meteorite research programs at the University of New Mexico and described numerous new meteorites, many of which he had personally recovered. He also, almost single-handedly, established the outstanding meteorite collection at the University of New Mexico and his research resulted in the publication of over 120 scientific articles and books, and he also helped establish the journal *Meteoritics* and served as President of the Meteoritical Society. La Paz died on 19 October 1985 in Albuquerque, New Mexico. **(12)**

According to Rickett, he and La Paz were given an assignment to determine "the speed and trajectory" of the object that impacted near Roswell. Rickett further imparted that he and La Paz had discovered a "possible touchdown point" about five miles northwest of the debris field located by rancher Brazel. Not only did they retrieve material identical to that which Rickett had handled before at the Foster Ranch, they were startled to find that the sand in the high-desert terrain had crystallized, apparently as a result of exposure to tremendous heat. Rickett and La Paz reportedly spent a total of three weeks interviewing witnesses and making their calculations, which were contained in an official report prepared by La Paz. Although Rickett never had a chance to see the document, which was delivered directly to the Pentagon, the professor confided to Rickett that, in his opinion and based upon all of the physical evidence they had collected and tested, the object was an "unmanned interplanetary probe." (13)

As far as the question of bodies is concerned, Randle and Schmitt's sources informed them that up to five were found in the vicinity of the crash site, one of which, incredibly, survived the initial impact. Among those that were willing to speak – albeit in a fragmented and cryptic fashion – were Edwin Easley, the Provost Marshal at Roswell, who made brief allusions to "the creatures;" Sergeant Melvin E. Brown, who stated that, "They looked Asian but had larger heads and no hair. They looked a yellowy color;" and the aforementioned Thomas Gonzalez, who described them as "little men." (14)

And still further accounts abound, including that of Dr. La June Foster, a renowned authority on the human spinal cord who had held a security clearance and who had worked undercover for the FBI during the Second World War.

According to the research of Schmitt and Randle, following the crash, Foster was flown to Washington, D.C., where she was asked to examine the spinal structures of the retrieved bodies, and reported that it was possible one had survived the initial impact, albeit in a critically injured state. Foster, too, described the bodies as being short, with oversized heads. Most disturbing of all, Foster was told that if she talked, she would be killed. (15)

A somewhat similar death-threat scenario came from Frankie Rowe, whose father was attached to the Roswell Fire Department in 1947. Rowe reports that her father confided in the family that he had seen both debris and bodies, including one live being: "[T]he one that was walking was about the size of a 10 year old child, and it didn't have any hair...it seemed so scared and lost and afraid." Several days later, claims Rowe, three military policemen came to the family home and said that if anyone talked, "they might just take us out to the middle of the desert and shoot all of us and nobody would ever find us." **(16)**

Similarly, consider the account of Glenn Dennis (of which even some pro-UFO researchers are highly suspicious, it must be noted), a mortician at Ballard's Funeral Home in Roswell, who claims to have received a strange telephone call from the mortuary officer at the base: "He was inquiring about what size, what type of caskets, and how small [were the] caskets that we could furnish that could be hermetically sealed," said Dennis.

Dennis also signed a sworn affidavit, confirming that a nurse friend at the base had admitted to him that a preliminary autopsy of the bodies had been conducted at Roswell Army Air Field: "[S]he went into this room to get some supplies and saw two doctors in there with a gurney and these small bodies that were in a rubber sheet or body pouch. Two of the bodies had been very badly mangled, like maybe the predators had been eating on them…one of the hands was severed from the body, and when they flipped it over, there were little tiny suction cups on the inside of the fingers…The heads were large, eyes were set in. The skulls were soft like a newborn baby's; they were pliable. The ears, instead of one canal, had two canals, no lobes or anything, just a little flap over each canal. The mouths were just very small slits. Their face and nose were concave." **(17)** And similar accounts abound.

In 1947, Lydia Sleppy was employed as a teletype-operator at the KSWS radio station in Roswell. When reporter Johnny McBoyle telephoned her with his account of seeing a "big crumpled dishpan" out on the Foster Ranch at 4.00 p.m. on Monday 7 July 1947, she recognized that this was a "pretty big story." Indeed it was. According to Sleppy's recollections, McBoyle added excitedly: "The Army is there and they are going to pick it up. And get this – they're saying something about little men being on board." Fifty years after the events in question,

McBoyle steadfastly declined to elaborate upon what it was that he saw on the Foster Ranch on that fateful day in July 1947. (**18**)

On the day following Johnny McBoyle's experience – 8 July 1947 – the FBI Office at Dallas, Texas, forwarded a Teletype message to FBI Director, J. Edgar Hoover concerning the events at Roswell. Notably, this is one of the very few officially declassified documents on the case that has surfaced under the terms of the Freedom of Information Act.

It is evident from examining the contents of the document that the FBI was only in possession of part of the story: that part had been supplied sometime previously by Major Edwin M. Kirton of Army Air Force Intelligence at Fort Worth. Indeed, an examination of the documentation at issue shows that even the FBI was fed the story that the "disc" recovered at Roswell was probably a weather balloon and was being forwarded to Wright Field for further examination as part of a concerted effort to confirm this hypothesis:

"Flying Disc, information concerning: Major Edwin E. Kirton, headquarters Eighth Air Force, telephonically advised this office that an object purporting to be a flying disc was recovered near Roswell, New Mexico, this date. The disc is hexagonal in shape and was suspended from a balloon by cable, which balloon was approximately twenty feet in diameter. Major Kirton further advised that the object found resembles a high altitude weather balloon with a radar reflector, but that telephonic conversation between their office and Wright Field had not borne out this belief. Disc and balloon being transported to Wright Field by special plane for examination. Information provided this office because of national interest in case and fact that National Broadcasting Company, Associated Press, and others attempting to break story of location of disc today. Major Kirton advised would request Wright Field to advise Cincinnati Office results of examination. No further investigation being conducted." (**19**)

There is an intriguing footnote to the story of the FBI's involvement in the Roswell controversy: in 1981 the researcher William Moore succeeded in tracking down the by-then-retired FBI agent who transmitted the aforementioned Teletype. The agent, however, refused to discuss the incident in any shape or form. Indeed, in a July 1988 lecture Moore graphically recalled the agent's words to him: "I have had no unexplained fires in my garage, and I have had no men in dark suits at my doorstep. I'm enjoying my retirement and I want to keep it that way, Mr. Moore. I have nothing to say to you." An unusual comment for sure, particularly if all that was recovered at Roswell was a weather balloon. **(20)**

Almost three decades after the late Major Jesse Marcel resurfaced with his story of what occurred at Roswell, accounts and testimony similar to that cited above continue to both circulate and mutate. In fact, the case has generated such interest that in the mid-1990s, and after nearly fifty years of deafening silence, the Air Force was finally forced to address the controversy: the battle between the believers and the sceptics was about to be taken to a whole new level.

1. *Roswell Daily Record*, 8 July 1947.
2. Information provided to the author by Stanton T. Friedman, 19 December 1993.
3. *The Roswell Incident: Beginning of the Cosmic Watergate*, Stanton T. Friedman and William L. Moore, MUFON Symposium Proceedings, 1981.
4. *The Roswell Incident*, Charles Berlitz and William L. Moore, Granada Publishing Ltd., 1980.
5. *The Roswell Investigation: New Evidence, New Conclusions*, William L. Moore, 1982.
6. Ibid.
7. *Crash at Corona*, Stanton T. Friedman and Don Berliner, Paragon House, 1992.
8. *The Roswell Incident*, Charles Berlitz and William L. Moore, Granada Publishing Ltd., 1980.

9. *Crashed Saucers: Evidence in the Search for Proof,* William L. Moore, MUFON Symposium Proceedings, 1985.

10. *The Truth About the UFO Crash at Roswell*, Kevin D. Randle and Donald R. Schmitt,

M. Evans, 1994. *UFO Crash at Roswell*, Kevin D. Randle and Donald R. Schmitt, Avon, 1991.

11. Ibid. *The Roswell Incident*, Charles Berlitz and William L. Moore, Granada Publishing Ltd., 1980. *UFO*, Vol. 9, No. 5.

12. www.math.ohio-state.edu/history/biographies/lapaz

13. *The Truth About the UFO Crash at Roswell*, Kevin D. Randle and Donald R. Schmitt,

M. Evans, 1994. *UFO Crash at Roswell*, Kevin D. Randle and Donald R. Schmitt, Avon, 1991.

14. Ibid. *Alien Liaison*, Timothy Good, Random Century Ltd., 1991. *Alien Contact*, Timothy Good, Morrow, 1992.

15. *The Truth About the UFO Crash at Roswell*, Kevin D. Randle and Donald R. Schmitt,

M. Evans, 1994. *UFO Crash at Roswell*, Kevin D. Randle and Donald R. Schmitt, Avon, 1991.

16. Ibid.

17. *Roswell in Perspective*, Karl Pflock, The Fund for UFO Research, 1994.

18. *Roswell in Perspective*, Karl Pflock, The Fund for UFO Research, 1994. *The Truth About the UFO Crash at Roswell*, Kevin D. Randle and Donald R. Schmitt,

M. Evans, 1994. *UFO Crash at Roswell*, Kevin D. Randle and Donald R. Schmitt, Avon, 1991. *The Roswell Incident*, Charles Berlitz and William L. Moore, Granada Publishing Ltd., 1980. *Crash at Corona*, Stanton T. Friedman and Don Berliner, Paragon House, 1992.

19. Federal Bureau of Investigation, 8 July 1947.

20. Lecture, July 1988.

VANDALS... Part I
by Robert E Vardeman

Charlie Benteen leaned forward and used an oil rag from his hip pocket to scrub at the inside of the windshield. The rough New Mexico desert road made his effort to clean the glass futile.

"Dammit, Charlie, stop messin' with that. You're only makin' it worse." Lew Schuster wiped his nose with his sleeve, then turned and spat out the window. Charlie cringed as most of the tobacco arched back into the rear seat of the lumbering DeSoto. He had spent the whole livelong day cleaning the green car and making it shine, then Lew had taken it into his head to go tearing out across the boondocks like this and getting the car all dirty again. Worse, he wouldn't stop chewing while he drove. Another arc of brown goo hit the air rushing past the car and came around through the open window into the back seat.

"You're makin' one hell of a mess."

"You act like this is your car or somethin'," Lew said.

"It's not yours, either."

"It's borrowed. Let's leave it at that."

"Old man Wilkinson don't know we took it for a joy ride. There'll be hell to pay when he finds out."

"So don't tell him," Lew said.

Charlie started to argue the point, then subsided and put the rag back into his overalls pocket. Lew was right about smearing the grime on the windshield. They were tearing along the potholed desert road at almost forty miles an hour and seeing through the dust cloud they kicked up behind them was nigh on impossible. A bit of oil smeared on the windshield didn't do anything to help and actually hurt the visibility when dust mixed with it in a splotch indistinguishable from Lew's gobbets of chaw.

"Why don't you turn on the headlights?"

Lew spat the final wad out the window. This time it was heavy enough to keep from curling back, but Charlie was sure it smooshed along the outside. He had taken special care washing the car for their boss as a way of thanking him for what he'd done. Ev Wilkinson was about the only man in Roswell who had the balls to give them a job. Lew had run into trouble with the law over in Socorro about a fight in a bar, and Charlie was still trying to convince folks that he hadn't helped himself to the cash register at the grocery store a couple months back. The trial kept getting postponed, but he was sure he could convince the judge it was all a big misunderstanding. Besides, the store had owed him the money in overtime and had refused to pay up because of his smeary time card. It wasn't stealing if you only took what was rightfully yours, he had decided a long time back.

Still, he had to watch his p's and q's until the trial, and he didn't like the way Lew was all furtive and close-lipped about why he wanted to go driving in the middle of the desert at this time of night. Charlie stuck his head out the window and looked up at the almost full moon. It was getting on toward fall soon, but the air ripping at his face still carried daggers of heat from the day, though the desert had cooled off plenty fast. In another hour when it got closer to midnight, it would be downright cold. He had lived in the Southwest long enough to know that away from the city out in the desert at night could get downright dangerous.

Charlie strained to hear the coyotes baying at the moon, but the rumble of the massive tires against the sun baked dirt drowned out any chance he had of that. It was just as well. Coyotes scared him after he had seen what a couple of them had done to a sickly calf.

"There it is. Up ahead," Lew said. He stomped on the brakes and the heavy car began slewing all over the road.

"What's up ahead?"

"I overheard Wilkinson say that the jeep had run out of gas."

"His new Willys?"

"New, like hell. It's a '46. That makes it a couple years old."

"Only a year. The new models ain't on sale yet and won't be for another month. He got that jeep up in Albuquerque, and it's his pride and joy. What's it doing out here?"

"Charlie, you're some kind of idiot. He was drivin' out here lookin' for who knows what and he run outta gas. Didn't you hear him this afternoon when he was all pissy about havin' to walk five miles 'fore he hitched a ride?" Lew jerked his thumb toward the backseat. Charlie looked hesitantly, knowing he would see the gobs of chaw everywhere. Instead, his eyes fixed on the red and yellow gallon gas can in the rear foot well.

"You're comin' out here to do him the favor of drivin' back?" Charlie had gotten to know Lew pretty well, and that didn't sound like him at all. The two of them had palled around for the past six months, listened to the jukebox at the Windsor Bar and Grille, playing it with nickels they had found out in the parking lot, and had tried to pick up women there. Lew was better at chatting up the girls but hadn't scored much, if at all, though to hear him tell it he was the biggest stud in the whole damned Tularosa Basin.

"What a sap," Lew said contemptuously. "It's almost a new jeep. What's it worth?"

"I dunno. Eight hundred dollars, maybe."

"Yeah, 'bout that," Lew said, scowling. "So for the price of a gallon of gas, we got ourselves a new jeep. We drive it south, sell it in El Paso for a couple hundred and 'fore we get back to Roswell it's over the border and sold somewhere in central Mexico."

"You mean steal it?"

"Yes, I mean steal it," Lew said sarcastically. "It's foolproof. There's nobody to say we done it. What's the matter? Can't use an extra hundred?"

"Well, sure, but the jeep belongs to old man Wilkinson, and he's treated us good. He gave us jobs at the garage when nobody else would."

"He works us like a rented mule, and you know it. He gets twice the mileage out of us than he would anybody else. This is our due, Charlie." Lew pulled to a full stop amid a choking cloud of dust, jerked the balky column-mounted gear shift to park and bailed out of the car before Charlie could think of a comeback.

He followed reluctantly, not wanting any part of it. But what Lew said was right. Nobody'd know they took the jeep, and nobody'd ever know they sold it in El Paso for a couple hundred dollars. Whether Lew was right about Wilkinson owning them the money for working so hard was something he'd have to think on.

"Get the gas can, will you?"

"Lew, this isn't right. We—"

Charlie threw up his arm to protect his face when a sudden flash of white light spotlighted him.

"Cops!"

"Ain't the cops," Lew said, trying to sound composed, but Charlie heard the quaver in his friend's voice. The flaring light had spooked him, too.

"Then what was it?"

"How should I know? Might be something from the base. Night maneuvers."

"You mean from the air field?"

"Yeah, the Roswell Army Air Field, you dummy. What else would it be?"

"It disappeared real quick. Wouldn't we see a plane or hear it?" Charlie cocked his head to one side and started to go back to the car. The sound wasn't anything like he'd heard in his life, and it came from over a sand hill not fifty yards away—in the direction of the blinding light. Yellow and blue spots still danced around in front of him, like somebody had popped a flashbulb in his face.

"You worry too damn much," Lew said. He rested his hand on the cold metal side of the Willys jeep, then pointed over the hill. "If it's eating you so much, go look while I fill the tank."

The way Lew challenged him made Charlie angry enough to start the long walk to the top of the sand dune so he could check out the low whirring sound. He couldn't look scared like he had after he had tried to talk his friend out of stealing their boss' jeep. Friends were hard to come by, and Lew would drop him like a hot potato if he backed down for an instant.

Charlie's mouth went dry when he reached the crest of the dune, and he would have turned and run if his feet would have obeyed. He froze in place, staring at the fifty-foot-diameter saucer-shaped craft slowly spinning a couple feet above the desert. From where he stood he couldn't see any legs supporting the silvery disk, but light poured through a rectangular opening on the underside, illuminating the greasewood, whip-like ocotillo and prickly pear cactus clumps with a light brighter than high noon.

"Jesus," Lew said behind him. "Look at that, will you?"

"What is it?"

"Damned if I know. I heard 'bout them rocket tests over at White Sands. This must be one of them built by our tame Germans."

"Don't look like anything I ever heard of," Charlie said, fascinated by the low hum, the metallic sheen and the way the gizmo rotated steadily in midair. He started down to get a closer look.

"Where you goin'? We gotta get the jeep gassed and outta here."

"So get the gas can. I won't be a minute." Charlie was surprised to see the fright on Lew's face. He hadn't thought his friend was scared of anything. He had even called out Big Billy Garson the other night, but the sheriff's deputy had busted it up before the fight got past pushing and shoving. Still, Big Billy had a reputation and folks said last year he had killed a steer with a single punch from his Mason-jar-sized right hand.

"Don't, Charlie. There ain't no reason to go closer to see things that you cain't see from here."

"Might be something I can steal. That'd sell for pretty penny." Charlie knew he was boasting, but this was about the first time he felt superior to Lew, who was always coming up with ideas like stealing Wilkinson's jeep and selling it. For once, he could lord it over his buddy. Charlie pulled free of Lew's grip on his arm and half-slid down the hill, avoiding the worst of the stickers and cactus thorns. At the base of the hill, he looked back and saw Lew silhouetted by the moon, making him look downright eerie. He waved, then went to see what this thing was making such a racket.

The closer he got the louder the hum. Along with the buzz that rattled his innards, Charlie heard clanking and hissing gases being released. He looked around and didn't see anything dangerous. He poked his head in the opening on the underside of the disk.

"Damnation," he exclaimed as he looked around. Somehow the inside of the slowly rotating disk was larger than its exterior. *Lots* larger. He could park the DeSoto and the jeep and a dozen other cars from Wilkinson's garage inside and have plenty of room left.

He didn't see anyone inside, so he gripped the edge of the opening and heaved himself up to sit with his feet dangling down. This should have been as far as he went, but Charlie remembered when he was a kid. He and a couple friends played on the grounds of a Carmelite monastery and had double dirty dog dared each other to go inside the monastery. His friend had taken the dare and disappeared inside. Charlie thought the stories of what all he had seen were lies, especially the part about the naked nun, but he could never prove it since he'd been too chicken to go himself.

Not now.

He swung his feet up and went exploring. He almost fell when he took a couple quick steps since he felt so light. Half his weight, maybe.

"Oh, hell, Lew's gonna piss his pants when I show him all this." Charlie went to a panel at the far side of the room that swept around in a long arc. Glittering crystals were embedded in the panel and strange squiggles like what a fourth grade teacher had told him were Egyptian hieroglyphics glowed in a dozen different colors. The rainbow of symbols changed constantly, but the gems in the board remained inert.

Charlie whipped out his pocket knife and pried loose one gemstone and held it up. It shimmered with an inner light.

"This is worth the price of the jeep," he decided. Working fast, he popped out a dozen of the diamonds or rubies or whatever the hell they were and stuffed them into his overalls pocket before going to stand by a table outfitted with clamps.

He shivered at this and didn't know why. It just didn't *feel* right. Charlie stepped back and almost fell.

"Put on a lot of weight real quick," he muttered, grabbing the edge of the table for support. He straightened and realized his weight was normal again. Rather than floating like a feather, his step was plodding.

More than his weight had changed. The panel where he had yanked out the gems now flashed its symbols at him in unison, as if it was gathering up a big anger. The dim lights inside were also flickering.

"Time to motor on outta here," he decided. He spoke to himself too loud, but it buoyed his courage and lent speed to his retreat to the doorway in the floor. He tried to find some way to close it up after him but couldn't see anything but the hole. He jumped, dropped and hit the ground under the now wobbling silvery disk. Tiny sparks sizzled and popped at the very edge, warning him something was going wrong with this gadget.

He scuttled out from under and stopped dead in his tracks. Ten feet away stood two creatures. At first Charlie thought coyotes had come to eat him. Huge yellow eyes stared unblinkingly at him, then he realized those eyes were too big for any coyote he had ever seen. And the eyes were almond shaped in creatures with ungainly heads and standing only four feet tall.

If somebody had lit the oily rag stuffed into his back pocket, Charlie Benteen could not have run faster up the hill and toward the jeep where Lew waited impatiently.

"It's about damn time," Lew said. "We gotta—"

"Run, Lew, run for your life!" Charlie vaulted into the jeep and savagely twisted the ignition key. Old man Wilkinson hadn't bothered to take it with him when he ran out of gas, probably because he was afraid of losing it like he did all the time.

The engine coughed and sputtered, then caught as fresh gasoline rushed through the carburetor. Charlie was torn between lifting the hood to adjust the timing and getting the hell away.

"I saw eyes, Lew. Huge eyes."

"What are you goin' on about?" Lew walked around to the side of the jeep, but Charlie wasn't giving up his spot behind the wheel.

Charlie crammed his foot down on the gas pedal and roared off when he heard a deeper, louder humming noise from over the hill. It wasn't right leaving Lew behind like that, but what did it matter? Lew had the DeSoto. Charlie hunkered down and floor boarded the accelerator until he was hitting bumps so hard he left the seat and only remained inside the jeep because of his death grip on the steering wheel. He wished he could shift out of four-wheel drive and go faster, but to do that he'd have to stop, manually turn the Warn hubs on the front wheels and get back to two-wheel drive. There wasn't time.

The humming became a whine so loud it hurt his ears.

A glance in the rearview mirror almost made Charlie's heart explode. The mirror was filled with flashing green and blue lights and the wobbly disk floating only feet off the road. Somehow, the immense rotating disk kept up without any wheels or propellers or jets or anything.

A second glance gave him a flash of relief when the disk disappeared. Then Charlie let out a scream as he looked directly overheard. The disk entirely filled the sky and blotted out the stars and moon and everything. Charlie's scream choked off when he felt invisible fingers tugging at him. Try as he might to hang onto the steering wheel, his grip weakened and he spun through the air, leaving the jeep on the ground as he sailed straight up.

Charlie thought he would smash into the disk's underside, but he didn't. Somehow a door opened and he flashed through it and the door closed under him and he hit the floor and felt the movement of the disk around him and . . .

. . . He stared into those unblinking yellow eyes again. Two creatures hardly four feet tall, with huge heads, spindly arms and a curious gray cast to their skin stared at him.

He screamed, but the sound was drowned out by grinding noises from somewhere deep inside the disk. One of the creatures reached out a hand with three fingers that moved as bonelessly as octopus tentacles.

"Suckers! You got suckers on them and you're gonna drink my blood."

Charlie screamed and tried to scuttle away as the one gray-skinned creature stepped toward him, raising his other hand. All Charlie could see were the tiny, twitching tendrils coming toward him to kill him.

He got his feet under him, put his head down and charged like a bull. He lost traction on the slick metal floor and flailed forward, arms outstretched. He grabbed and caught the wrist of the alien closest to him and pulled down hard. Bones or something passing for bones snapped under Charlie's grip and then the tendrilled hand popped free, leaving him staring in mute horror at the twitching member.

The two aliens scuttled back, dragging their feet. Charlie saw they were naked but what he expected to see wasn't apparent on their bodies.

"Look, ladies, I didn't mean nuthin' by this." He held out the convulsing hand toward them. The tendrils were wilting visibly, looking like ferns left in the hot New Mexico sun. "You gotta believe I didn't mean to hurt you. You scared me. If your menfolk are around, I can explain everything to them."

The two aliens huddled together, heads pressed close. Charlie didn't hear any sounds from them. It was as if they were afraid of him because he had maimed the one. This gave him a surge of courage. He stood and waved the now brown, fragile hand at them angrily.

"You didn't have no call doin' this to me. You snatched me from Mr. Wilkinson's jeep. I don't know what happened when I wasn't behind the wheel anymore. It coulda been wrecked, for all I know. And this!" He shook the hand again. "You tried to attack me. You got what you deserved attackin' me, havin' your hand ripped off." This time when he waved the severed hand around, it turned to dust and left a greasy smear on his palm. Charlie took out his rag and wiped frantically to get the spot off.

He settled down when he scoured all of the alien blood off his hand and tucked the rag into his pocket.

"You let me outta here right now. You got no call imprisonin' me. Only the cops can do that." When he got no response, he shuffled nervously, licked his lips and shouted, "I'll call the damn sheriff myself if you don't let me go right now!"

He waved his fist in the air. Charlie never saw what happened because the two aliens did not move so much as a muscle, but powerful invisible hands gripped his waist and upended him in the air. Spinning about an axis several feet off the floor, he tried to get back to the floor, slippery as it was.

"You let me down right now. How are you holdin' me in thin air like this? You can't do this!" Charlie screamed again when he floated slowly toward the table he had seen on his first entry into the disk. He tried to swim like he would in a stock tank. The air wasn't thick enough for him to get any traction. He drifted closer to the table. Then support went away and he fell heavily facedown onto the table.

Charlie fought but couldn't move fast enough to avoid the clamps on his ankles and wrists that automatically closed.

"What are you doing? You perverts!" He tried kicking but could not move as his overalls were pulled down. His underwear sizzled and popped and disappeared, leaving him bareass. Then he began screaming in earnest as he felt something cold and slick and round poking about his hindquarters. Charlie tensed his butt but could not keep the cylinder from entering. For a few seconds, he thought this was all the humiliation he had to endure.

"Hell, ladies, this ain't no worse 'n when the jocks on the football team depantsed me my first year in high school." He laughed because that had been his only year in high school, and then he screamed until he was hoarse.

Electricity jangled, gently at first and then with increasing voltage until Charlie lay twitching uncontrollably on the table, his body filled with excruciating pain such as he had never experienced in his life. Not even when he had broken his collarbone trying to impress Ruth Ann Mathis in the eighth grade with his inadequate gymnastic talents had he felt such agony.

He wasn't sure how long the torture continued because he blacked out. The next thing he knew was almost drowning in a puddle of his own sweat and blood. He turned his head to the side to avoid the pool formed by his own fear and a lip bitten almost clean through in his convulsive thrashing.

Eyes blurry, he blinked hard and focused on the two aliens at the arc of lights and flashing hieroglyphics. Unlike when he had left the disk before, the colors had returned to a rainbow variety and all the jewels he had swiped glimmered again in their proper holes.

"You sons o' bitches." He blinked harder and cleared his eyes, then remembered what he had discovered about the two aliens when he got a good look at their crotches. "Bitches!" He tried to shout the insult but only gurgled because of the blood filling his mouth. A tooth might have fallen victim to their torture from the way everything hurt.

The two aliens glided back and forth, reaching out to touch the gems with their tendrils. For a second, Charlie couldn't figure out what was wrong. Then it hit him. Both of them had all their hands. He couldn't identify the one whose hand he had ripped off, but both of the aliens had all their limbs now. The idea that the disk carried more than the pair he watched chilled him. This might be some kind of invasion, though where it came from—where the two little female aliens came from—was a complete mystery.

Charlie didn't care a whit for that. He had endured a shaft run up his rear and then plugged into an electrical outlet. Getting away before they carried out more of their sick perversions mattered most. Arching his back was easier than he expected because his weight had decreased, and he felt as light as when he had first entered the disk.

Moving slowly to keep from making a noise the aliens might hear, he turned onto his side and began putting all the force he could against his right manacle. Try as he might he couldn't budge it. In frustration, he slammed the cuff down against the table. To his surprise it popped open, freeing his hand. Frantic now, he repeated the procedure on the left manacle and got it off, too. Naked from the waist down, he reared up on his knees and almost passed out. The probe was still rammed all the way up his rear end. Charlie reached back and yanked it out, then got to work on his ankle chains. They opened the same way, with a sudden tap against the table.

He fell backward off the table and sat on the floor, panting harshly. Fearfully, he looked around the table to be sure they hadn't heard him. Both were more animated now, hurrying from side to side and touching the glowing jewels with what might have been anxiety.

Charlie crawled on hands and knees to the spot where he had been brought into the disk and looked around frantically for a way to open the door. In frustration he pounded his fists on the bare floor.

The solid floor vanished, and he was falling through the air, screaming as he went. He crashed to the ground and screamed again. His bare ass had landed on a barrel cactus. Scrambling to his feet, he danced around and then looked up to see the disk glowing a pale green. It spun faster and faster and then flashed away so fast all it left behind was a memory of light in his eyes.

Then he saw a second glowing light in the sky. It hovered some distance away, high up, and he was sure it was hunting for him. Then he saw the first disk so far up in the night sky he could hardly make it out, but it was moving and green and obviously didn't belong. The second disk tilted and simply disappeared.

Charlie stared at the empty New Mexico sky for several minutes, relieved that he had escaped and fearful they would come back for him. With two of the disks and their weird ways of lifting him off his feet and him being bareass and all he could not hope to escape.

They didn't come back, but he did hear a powerful engine and the crunch of tires on the sunbaked tracks.

Lew Schuster drove up in the DeSoto, skidded to a halt and leaned out the window to stare at him. Lew started to say something, stopped, then finally said, "You're not wearing pants."

"Yeah, I know." Charlie looked over his shoulder into the sky but saw nothing that shouldn't be there.

"Well, get into the car, pervert."

Charlie dropped into the seat, riding shotgun no longer meaning much to him. The cactus spines tore at his butt but nothing like he had experienced before.

"You wrecked the jeep," Lew said, staring ahead with such intensity the veins stood out in his neck.

"We'll tell Wilkinson we came out to get it for him and found it that way."

Lew said nothing until he put the car into gear and pulled away, heading toward the distant lights of Roswell sparkling in the middle of the desert.

"Why say anything at all? Let him find it and wonder."

"Okay."

"What are we going to say if anybody sees us drivin' back together, you not wearin' any pants?"

"Let them all wonder about that, too," Charlie said. He craned his neck out the window and scanned the sky. Nothing unusual. Good. Very good and to hell with trying to find his overalls with the pockets full of diamonds and rubies. He'd had enough larceny for one night.

To be continued...
In VANDALS... Part II

EIGHTEEN
by Jean Rabe

The old man smelled bad—thick with the acrid, fusty scents of raggedy clothes crusted with food stains and arthritis balm that had been spread on recently and too liberally. Not even sitting on the wide front porch rimmed by geraniums and snapdragons, with big baskets of petunias hanging from posts—all of that being stirred by the summer breeze—wasn't enough to cover the old-man odors.

Zachary wrinkled his nose, summoned his resolve, and moved closer. He gently placed a hand on the old man's knee.

"It's good to see you, Grandpa," he said.

Robert James Collins, oblivious to his guest, fiddled with the top button of his shirt. The plaid flannel was frayed at the collar and the wrists and would have been far too warm for someone with proper circulation. His skin, yellowed and flaking, was clearly not washed often enough anymore; his eyes were rheumy and the left one was discolored as if from a cataract.

"It's good to see you, Grandpa," Zachary repeated, this a little louder.

"Nice to see you, Zeek," he finally answered.

Zach, Zachary mouthed.

"Been a while, Zeek. Hasn't it?" Robert dropped his hands to his lap and stared forward.

"I was here just last week, Grandpa," Zachary lied. "Don't you remember?" In fact, he hadn't been by to visit since eight months past, when Robert hadn't looked quite so frail as today. And he'd visited only once before that, two and a half years ago, when the old man's eyes were brighter and his memory a hair better. "Don't you remember that I brought you some lemonade? And a big box of Twinkies?"

Robert pursed his lips and continued to stare forward. "I like Twinkies. Did you bring me some today?"

Zachary shook his head. "I'll remember to bring two boxes next time. I'll remember. I promise."

"I don't remember a lot, Zeek. It's that . . ."

Alzheimer's, Zachary thought. Grandpa had been labeled with it almost five years ago, the diagnosis safely landing him in this place.

"It's that damn illness they say I have. I hear them talking behind my back, the nurses. There's nothing much wrong with my hearing. I can hear 'em all talking."

Zachary knew that Robert Collins was eighty, soon to be eighty-one. But he looked much, much older—at least one hundred to Zachary's eyes. He'd been around people in their seventies and eighties often enough, all of them more . . . vital . . . than Robert Collins. A smelly husk of a man. A walking skeleton with age-spotted skin that looked painfully stretched over his brittle bones. Zachary felt sorry for him.

"But I remember some things," Robert added. "I remember that you joined the Army."

Air Force, Zachary mouthed.

"I'm remembering things today at least." He brushed at a line of drool that had spilled over his lower lip and turned so he could see Zachary. "Numbers do it, get me to remembering. They stir my brain, the numbers do."

"That's what the nurses told me when I called to check on you this morning. They said that you were chattering up a storm, talking about the nineteen forties as if they were only yesterday. In fact—" Zachary paused when a nurse in a pink frock came out on the porch, bringing two glasses of ice water for them and a blood pressure cuff. She fitted the cuff around Robert's arm, taking a reading over the flannel. When she was finished, she disappeared back inside and Zachary continued. "In fact, one of the nurses said you were talking about flying saucers in the New Mexico desert and—"

"Saucer," Robert corrected. "There was just ever the one that I picked up after. Rumor had it there were three crashes at different times. But I was just involved with the one."

"At Roswell."

The old man nodded. "Of course at Roswell." Another line of drool spilled out and dripped down to darken a spot on his shirt. He seemed not to notice. "It was July when the saucer crashed."

Zachary frowned. "You remember that?"

"July."

"Just like it is now, Grandpa. July."

"Hotter than hell, it was, in Roswell. July, it was. Did I say that, July? The nurses here don't believe me. Think it's my illness talking. The young Mexican one indulges me, though. She's *ding how* as far as I'm concerned, a real sweetie. None of the old folks here believe me either. Meatballs, all of them. But you believe me, don't you Zeek?"

"That's why I'm here," Zachary said softly. Louder: "Why don't you tell me about it, Grandpa? I've always been interested in stuff like that, UFOs and science fiction. I even watched that "alien autopsy" TV show that Jonathan Frakes narrated some years back. Why don't you—"

Robert was staring at something far beyond the porch and the flowers. Zachary gently squeezed his knee to regain his attention.

"I'd like to hear about it, Grandpa. Tell me all about Roswell and the crash."

"The crash that I cleaned up after? I'm glad someone wants to hear it. You're a good boy to pay attention to an old man. You and that young Mexican nurse. She called the *Plain Dealer* for me a few hours ago and talked to an editor there. She told me a reporter would come by tomorrow or the next day, tomorrow most likely 'cause she got the editor real interested. Hope it's a good one, the reporter, one that'll get my story right. The truth needs to come out about Roswell."

Zachary squeezed the old man's knee again. "I want to hear the story, Grandpa. All of it. I've got time today. I want to hear it from you, not read about it in the newspaper."

"Wish you would have brought some Twinkies." Robert grinned sadly. "It was 1947. I'm good with numbers, I am. Have problems with names and faces, at least nowadays. Have problems remembering a lot of things, Zeek. My illness. But numbers, those stay with me. Did I tell you that? About being good with numbers? I was eighteen in early July, 1947. Nineteen soon after, but eighteen when it began." He drew his face forward until it looked agonizingly pinched. "Numbers stir up old memories." Softer: "Bad ones from Roswell."

"What do you remember, Grandpa?" Zachary pressed.

"Eighteen." Robert's face relaxed and he leaned against the back of the wooden rocking chair. He looked comfortable, even though Zachary considered the stiff porch furniture anything but.

"It was in the Capitan Mountains in 1947, early July, or maybe the last day of June. Did I tell you it was summer? Hotter there than it ever gets here." A pause. "Where are we?"

"Ohio."

"Yeah, hotter than it ever gets in Shady Elm, Ohio."

Zachary raised an eyebrow. The previous visit, the old man hadn't mentioned the Capitan Mountains or New Mexico. He hadn't known what states he had lived in, let alone the name of this rest home—Shady Elm Retirement Center, just south of Dayton. Robert's mind was miraculously less foggy today.

"The Capitan Mountains weren't far outside of Roswell, Zeek. I was in them more than once, the last time on a hike with . . ." Robert rubbed at his lower lip, clearly trying to remember the name of at least one companion. "Anyway, I'd been in the mountains. We were all a bunch of cueballs. Paddlefoots they called us. Little more than fresh recruits."

"Near Roswell."

"Yes, near Roswell." Robert's voice picked up strength. "The desert sky was bright blue, cloudless on the day of the forced march."

"Sixty-two years ago," Robert whispered.

"There were a dozen of us, with just under a year in the service. We were in full gear and sweating so much the beads on our faces were the size of small coins. It was a dry heat, a lot different than the muggy heat here, and the air was so still it didn't stir a single strand of our hair . . . not that we had all that much to stir, the buzz cuts they gave us back then."

Robert chuckled at his last comment and ran his free hand over his mostly-bald head. "We had the permission of the J. B. Foster Ranch to cross the property that bordered this section of the mountains. I'd met with the foreman—W.W. "Mac" Brazel—the day before. Mac would play an important role in what would soon transpire.

"At one point the sky was full of birds. Big black ones that looked like hastily made charcoal smudges. The birds were quiet, though, and the only sound we heard was the crunch of our boots against the scree. Maybe there was something else in the sky besides black birds, bigger and higher and invisible to our eyes. Something that would come to ground soon enough, probably that very night."

Robert shook his head. "I remember that it was a long hike, the muscles burning like fire in my legs, my size elevens blistered from the sweat and from the trek. It was worse than basic training. I had the following day off, and I spent a good chunk of it on my backside in my bunk reading Thomas Calvert McClary's *Rebirth* and putting lotion on my soles.

"We should have marched just a little farther and a little longer, stayed out during that night. Would've seen it come down if we had, the saucer. I was eighteen," Robert said. He shook his head as if to clear the image. "Joined the Army when I was seventeen. Dad was okay with it and signed the papers. The war was over and so I figured it was safe to enlist. Didn't expect to be sent to hot-as-hell New Mexico. Didn't expect the aliens to come either."

A silence settled on the porch, and Robert watched a butterfly dance from petunia to petunia. When it had drank its fill and flew away, he continued.

"Mac was on horseback two days later, looking for some sheep that had scattered during the previous night's sudden thunderstorm. He found some unusual debris strewn across a pasture and plucked up a few choice pieces, passing them around to neighbors and to Chaves County Sheriff George Wilcox, who guessed that the wreckage came from something launched from the Roswell Army Air Field. But we hadn't launched anything. I was eighteen that year, did I mention that, Zeek? Turned nineteen later, but eighteen when it started."

"Eighteen, yes, Grandpa. You mentioned that a few times."

"Eighteen is three sixes, and that's the devil's mark. I'm a religious man, always was, and so the sixes bother me. The devil played a role in what happened in Roswell. All hell broke loose there that July."

Zachary finished his water and sat the glass between his feet. He noticed the old man hadn't touched his drink, just held it in his right hand.

"Do you want me to hold that for you, Grandpa? So you don't drop it?"

The old man didn't answer, still caught up in the memory.

The wood groaned as a nurse wheeled a short woman in a baggy seersucker dress out. Robert scowled at the nurse, mouthing something. The nurse got the message and took her patient to the other side of the sweeping porch.

"Major Marcel was in charge, right, Grandpa?" Zachary prompted. "Of the Roswell crash?"

Robert's scowl deepened. "Bad with names, I told you, Zeek." He made a tsk-tsking sound as if scolding a child. "My illness, you know. Surprised I remember Mac from the ranch. Don't even remember who I reported to, someone in the 509th Bomb Group. Someone tall with bushy eyebrows you wanted to pluck and yellowed teeth that were crooked in front. But I remember he put me on the crew picking up the debris, cleaning up the devil's handiwork. July 8th . . . another number for you, Zeek . . . the local paper that day said what we picked up was pieces of a flying saucer. The reporter was right, but the Army denied it. Bet they're still denying it."

"A weather balloon, Grandpa, that's what the Army press releases called it back then . . . and that's what the Army still calls it now. Maybe that's all it ever was, some fancy weather balloon."

Robert's mouth worked as if he was chewing on something. "Weather balloon, hell."

"But—"

"Oh, you watched them television programs, eh? History Channel or whatnot, Zeek? Or did you read some book?"

Zachary absently nodded. "I read a lot."

"Wasn't no damn weather balloon that came down in the desert." The old man ran the fingers of his free hand around the lip of his glass. "There's a museum out there, in Roswell. All built around Area 51. Never saw it, the museum. Hell, heard they have all sorts of alien-themed establishments there—restaurants and souvenir shops and hotels. Built them long after I was done in the Army, and I never had a cause to return to Roswell or Area 51."

"Another number," Zachary mused. "Area 51."

"I'm good with numbers. I remember about the press releases, too, the ones the Army wrote. The numbers jarred all that loose. Eighteen did it. They moved me down the hall from where I was, wanting to do some painting in my old room. Moved me into Room 18, and it jarred everything loose."

"Eighteen," Robert repeated.

"Three sixes."

"The devil's handiwork, Grandpa."

"A weather balloon and its radar reflector, the releases said." Robert smirked. "If it was just a balloon we wouldn't have had to contact . . . to contact . . ." His face brightened suddenly, erasing a few of the years. "Ballard! To contact the Ballard Funeral Home to get some small caskets and to learn how to preserve bodies that had been left outside for a handful of days. Wouldn't have had base personnel autopsy a radar reflector, now would we? The Ballard Funeral Home, I remember the name of the place. I remember! We needed their advice for how to handle the alien corpses."

Zachary's expression clouded and he leaned closer. "Did you see what they autopsied, Grandpa? These so-called aliens?"

"Eighteen, Zeek. That number jarred it all loose."

"The three sixes."

"The devil's mark, Zeek. I saw the aliens, I did. See them now, in the back of my mind, all blue-gray—more blue than gray—and looking old and young at the same time, big black bug-eyes, swollen heads. They had skinny arms and legs and knobby knees, long fingers that looked like spider legs."

"Just like the images in the museum," Zachary mused.

"Never saw what they put in the museum. But I know they looked just like the aliens from 1897."

"What?" Zachary sucked in a deep breath.

"You think I'm nuts, don't you?"

"No, Grandpa, it's just that—"

"I wasn't around that long ago, in 1897, but I read about it."

"1897?"

"They called it the Aurora Encounter. Four-seventeen, April seventeenth. Good with numbers, remember?"

"I remember. Go on." Zachary looked confused. "I thought we were talking about 1947 and Roswell."

"I'll get back to that. But like I said, I read about it, the 1897 crash. I was into science fiction at the time, when I was stationed at Roswell, and I saw an article about the Aurora Encounter when I was at the library seeing if they had anything new come in. Instead, I found the old newspaper clippings. It was an airship, the Texas Airship the article called it. And they found a body in it, alien like the ones from the desert. The description of the body pretty much matched what I saw . . . big bug eyes, spider-leg fingers. And I saw them up close. Same race come to call on us, I guess. Both times they had accidents with their flying saucers. And both times we tried to cover it up so the public wouldn't know."

Zachary's curiosity swelled. "Aliens. You saw them? You *really* saw them?"

"From the 1947 crash. Yeah, I saw the aliens from the Roswell desert. Some of them were in pieces from the impact. They smelled funny, like melting plastic. But I couldn't tell anybody about it then. Couldn't say a word. I'd promised. I was sworn to secrecy. And I was afraid to break my word. Afraid for my life."

"And now?"

"I'm telling you, ain't I, Zeek? Might as well tell it all while I can still remember. Get it all out. I'll tell that *Plain Dealer* reporter tomorrow, too. Gotta set the truth out there while I'm still breathing. I'm old enough I don't have anything to fear anymore. What are they gonna do, the Army? Kill me?"

"I'd really like to hear it, Grandpa. All of it. Like I said, I don't want to wait to read about it in the newspaper."

"Eighteen," Robert said. "In the eighteen days after the Roswell crash people were moved around, transferred, disappeared. Really disappeared. Sent to posts overseas."

"A cover-up."

"Obviously. I was smart enough to keep my mouth shut. Or maybe more likely I was just too scared at the time to open my yap. That stuff we picked up . . ."

"The stuff from the crash?"

"I wasn't wearing gloves that day, none of the gatherers were. Back then, people weren't so concerned about fingerprints and the like, and there'd been no thought given to whether anything was contaminated and might hurt us. The Army simply wanted everything retrieved as fast as possible."

"I can imagine."

"The day we collected the debris was not quite as hot as when we'd hiked into the mountains. There were gray-bellied clouds, hinting at more rain, and there was a reasonable breeze. We chatted as we worked, but I couldn't tell you now what we talked about—beyond speculating just what it was we bagged and boxed.

"It weighed less than nothing, the metal from the ship, less than a piece of tissue paper," he said, gesturing with his free hand. "I kept a little piece of it, a few of us kept some. Don't know where it is, though, my piece. In a box, maybe, with things from my old house. Maybe tossed, somebody did, not knowing what it was. Maybe it's even in the shoe box in my closet. Hadn't considered that possibility before now. It didn't weigh anything. So thin and silver, like tinfoil you'd see inside a cigarette pack. But it wasn't tinfoil. It didn't bend. Maybe it's in the closet in my room."

Robert fixed a faraway stare on Zachary. "The piece I pinched? I wedged it under the leg of my bunk that night and tried to bend it that way. Couldn't, though, not even a corner of it. After I was long-gone from Roswell, back at my parents' house, I took it out in the backyard and hit it with a wrench, then with a sixteen-pound sledge hammer. Didn't put a mark on it. Couldn't cut it, couldn't scratch it." He let out a raspy breath. "And it still didn't bend. Wish I knew what had become of it. I'd show it to the folks around here, and then maybe someone would believe my story. Think I'll have to check my closet when I go back inside. If it's there, I want the *Plain Dealer* reporter to see it. Did I tell you the saucer crashed in July?"

Zachary rested his head against the chair back. "I believe you, Grandpa. Somehow, I believe all of it. No weather balloon."

"You're a good boy, Zeek. Next time bring those Twinkies." Robert made a sound approximating a chuckle. "Eighteen. Three sixes."

"The devil's number."

Robert finally took a sip from his water glass and stared at his wrinkled reflection in the surface. "I was eighteen, Zeek. Did I mention that? I'd been trained to drive a jeep and some of the bigger Army trucks, but nothing quite as big as that eighteen-wheeled monstrosity I was assigned to when they decided to cart it all away from Roswell and the prying eyes of the reporters and the locals. You had to climb up to sit in the cab. The seats were leather and cracked, but it wasn't an old truck by a long stretch, just been beaten down by whoever had been using it."

"It wasn't an Army truck?"

"Hell no. They didn't want it to look like an Army operation. The cab was a drab olive green, a small patch of rust near the bottom of the driver side door looking like a butterfly's wing. The semi-trailer stretching behind it had a logo, three ears of corn tied together with a blue ribbon, icicles dripping from all of it. 'Nature's Very Best,' it read. 'Frozen Fresh From the Field.' It was a Timpte refrigeration trailer, new and direct from the manufacturing and service facility the company had opened recently in Albuquerque, New Mexico. The Timpte company had a history with the Army, having shipped textile trailers, laundry trailers, flatbeds, and refrigeration units to Europe and other theatres of war. The company had earned the Army-Navy "E" Award for excellence and provided the refrigeration trucks so that food could be transported to the soldiers during WWII."

Robert said he wasn't driving. "Not yet, anyway. Though I was going to take a shift at it soon, probably within the hour, just outside of Tulsa. I'd been dozing on and off since we'd left the base. The trip—well more than thirteen hundred miles—would take at least twenty-four hours because of the route they'd chosen for us, and the sergeant currently driving told me to rest so I'd be fresh for my turn at the wheel. Resting was difficult, though, as I couldn't get completely comfortable on the stiff seat. And I was sweating something fierce . . . from nerves and the summer heat. Nerves mostly, I guess. I was pretty worried over the cargo."

"The dead aliens."

"We needed the refrigeration trailer because of the alien corpses we were hauling," he said. "We needed to keep them cold to preserve them. Didn't want them rotting more than some of them already had. Ours wasn't the only truck headed from the Roswell base to Dayton. There were two others, considerably smaller and reading "Redwall Carpets" on the sides, and four cars that frequently changed positions, weaving between the trucks and staying in contact regularly and trying not to look suspicious. No one was in uniform, and nothing hinted that this was a military operation."

Robert lowered his voice to a conspiratorial whisper. "I was so happy to be involved in something covert and important. I thought it might net me a bump in rank. But the larger part of me wished I hadn't become involved at all. I wished I'd been oblivious to the crash in the desert and the contents of the 'Nature's Very Best' semi-trailer. I wished he'd never set foot in New Mexico."

Robert dabbed at his forehead. "It was hotter then, back in New Mexico and Oklahoma. The air washed in through the open truck windows and brought some grit with it. I spit sand. There was a radio in the truck, but Sarge had turned it off after the first half-hour, finding nothing to his musical taste that wasn't too static-filled and not caring about the local news. Rosemary Clooney, Artie Shaw, Count Basie. Sarge didn't care for any of them. Not even good old swinging Dizzy Gillespie. Said he wanted to hear the Dorsey Brothers and Bing Crosby. Turned it off in the middle of Cab doing some scat." Robert brushed a hand in front of his face, as if to clear away a cobweb. "Odd that I remember the singers. Things from long ago come a little clearer."

"Things seem to be coming pretty clear to you today, Grandpa."

"The caravan didn't take the main highways, and one of the cars often drifted back to make sure that no one was following us. Paranoia ran high. The reporters in New Mexico had been skeptical about the weather balloon story, and a few had been hovering at the fringes of the base trying to get a different take. But apparently none of them had caught wind of the secret caravan that was whisking every scrap of metal and every alien limb away from Roswell and to an Air Force base in the heart of the Midwest.

"Did you hear something?" Robert asked, so caught up in memory that he was repeating something he'd said sixty-two years past. "Did you hear something? I heard something, Sarge. I know I did. Listen. There it goes again. Really, it's not nothing, Sarge. I heard something. Honest. A thump. There! There it is again, I say. Good, you heard it, too." Robert stretched forward, fingers of his left hand closing on air, where they had closed on the mike long decades past. "Yes, sir. I'll call the lieutenant right away for . . ."

Robert closed his mouth and straightened his shoulders. It was several moments before he spoke again.

"The truck veered to the right, as if it had hit a patch of ice, though this wasn't the time of year or the place for it. I spotted sparks out the window, flying from wheels that had locked up and rims that were slicing through the tires. I felt my stomach rise into my throat and was suddenly speechless. The mike fell and struck my knee just as Sarge tried to compensate and steer to the left. The chatter of static and men barking questions over the two-way filled the air, I remember clear as a bell, competing with the high-pitched screams of the rims contacting the blacktop. Steam started hissing out of the engine as the truck lurched to the right again, hitting the ditch and flipping on its side, skidding across a field of soybeans. It was hell. The devil at work."

Robert sucked in his lower lip. "They didn't have seatbelts then." The water glass shook, and he held it with both hands now so he wouldn't drop it. "Me and the sergeant, we were bounced around pretty good that night. He fell into me . . . after he hit his head against the wheel and broke his jaw and got half his teeth knocked out. I couldn't breathe, him pressing me against the door. But somehow I managed to get out from under him. He wasn't dead, not at the moment. He died later, I was told, after we put him in one of the cars and tried to get him to a Tulsa hospital. I'd broken a couple of ribs, and my face was sliced up pretty bad. But I didn't even get a medic to look at me. We were too busy. Too much happened too fast."

The old man fell silent, again looking at something far beyond the porch of the Shady Elm Retirement Home.

"Don't stop, Grandpa," Zachary said. "Tell me the rest." He took the glass out of Robert's hands, noticing that the old man's knuckles were white.

Several more moments passed before the old man spoke again.

"Somehow I got out of the cab, climbed up the seat and out through the driver's side window. The other two trucks had stopped up on the road a ways back, and I could only see three of the cars. I found out later that the fourth car was wrecked in the opposite ditch. It had been hit by pieces of our truck that had come loose." He swallowed hard. "These are memories that were better left buried, Zeek. Bad memories, I told you."

"Grandpa?"

"It was the aliens, Zeek. They did it, caused our truck to go all out of control. Not all of the aliens were dead. Hurt? Yeah, hell yeah they were hurt, but the refrigeration . . . somehow it helped them. Scuttle later was that the cold rejuvenated them, that low temperatures were natural for them and that when they had crashed the desert heat had siphoned their strength. The ones that hadn't died in the crash were in some sort of suspended animation, and they'd woken up on the road between Roswell and

Tulsa, rejuvenated in the refrigeration trailer. We weren't far from Tulsa when they must have used whatever technology we'd stored in the trailer with them to lock up our wheels and kill the engine. Then they tried to kill all of us."

Again the old man stopped speaking, his throat working and his fingers clenching and unclenching. Zachary opened his mouth to urge him to continue, but Robert started again on his own accord. Zachary stared at the glass.

"The others from the base ran toward the back of the truck before I could get there. It had taken me a while to climb out and get my bearings. I was dizzy, hurting, had a little trouble staying on my feet. Everything was surreal, like in the science fiction books I liked to read. The dirt smelled burnt, smoke and steam poured out of the engine, and then I heard our lieutenant . . . I can't recall his name . . . he was shouting and pointing. Others were shouting, too. And then came this hissing, like a snake, but loud. And a crackling, like a live wire flapping against the pavement. There were more sparks, but this time they came from the back of the truck, and they were bright green. It looked like lightning, the angry fingers that come before a big summer storm."

Robert's knees wobbled. "I saw soldiers in plainclothes clutching their chests as bolts of hellish green lighting jumped from the back of the flipped trailer. The air was thick with ozone and blood, scorched dirt and the burnt plastic smell the aliens gave off. I could hardly breathe from the stink and the heat. The soldiers who managed to survive that first onslaught returned fire. Every soldier in the caravan had at least one weapon, and I dug at the small of my back for mine," he said.

"We weren't supposed to look military. So our guns were hidden, in pockets, strapped to our ankles. Only the lieutenant had a rifle, and he was one of the first to fall. I remember wanting to get to that rifle, then seeing someone go for it first and getting cut down by that green lightning. Angry fingers. Everything smelled so awful. I finally made it to the back of the trailer, just as one of the blue-tinged aliens came out from behind the cover of the broken door. I didn't hesitate, my training kicking in. Despite the pain in my ribs, I raised my gun and fired, blowing a hole in the back of the first alien's head, and yet not dropping him."

"It didn't die?"

"It screamed, but it wasn't a human sound. It was more like metal gears straining and grinding, high-pitched and hurtful. It screamed again when I fired a second time, striking it in the chest now, as it had spun around. A third bullet hit it in the head again, and finally the creature fell. I'd never killed anyone . . . anything . . . before. Never thought I'd have to, the war in Europe being over and all. But I killed something that night. Killed two of them, at least. Someone else, I can't remember his name, got two more. Then everything was quiet, except for the hissing of the truck engine, and a distant siren."

"The police?"

"County Sheriff," Robert corrected. "The crash, all the noise. Some farmer must have heard and called the sheriff's department. Made us work fast to load what we could into the other trucks and the cars. We stuffed alien corpses into the trunk of the big Chevy. What wouldn't fit, we set fire to. Even our fallen. Went up quick, everything did, what with the fuel tank nearly full on the semi."

The old man closed his eyes and drew his lips into a thin line. "We never accounted for one of the aliens, Zeek. Don't know if he escaped or burned up. If he escaped, he couldn't have lived for long in the Oklahoma heat. Maybe coyotes got him. Maybe his bones are buried in a soybean field on the far side of Tulsa."

"That's quite a tale, Grandpa."

"It didn't end there, Zeek." He opened his eyes. "We got out of there quick, not wanting to talk to the sheriff. We took back roads and went faster than we should have, only stopping for gas before we reached Dayton. Peeing in bottles."

"Dayton. The Air Force Base?"

"Wright-Patterson they called it after a fashion. Wright for ..."

"The Wright Bothers."

"Yeah. I remember that name. Wright-Patterson. The base was the repository for all manner of enemy aircraft that had been captured in World War II. The repository for pieces of the alien's craft, too. Hell, maybe other saucers were at the base. Maybe from the Aurora Encounter. Who knows? Hanger 18, that's where all of our pieces ended up, Zeek. I saw them all laid out in Hanger 18."

"Eighteen," Zachary breathed.

"Three sixes, the devil's number," Robert said. "The devil's handiwork I did back then."

"Funny that you remember all of this now. You never mentioned any of this when I stopped by before."

The old man shrugged. "Maybe you should have come by more often. They put me in Room 18, Zeek. That triggered all of it, I told you. Room 18. Hangar 18. I was eighteen. Three sixes. The devil was at work. You know, I heard they opened a bar in Dayton some years ago, called it Hangar 18. The rumors had followed the debris from Roswell to Ohio. You said we're in Ohio, right Zeek?"

"Shady Elm." Zachary nodded.

"Thought so. You're a good boy to come visit me, Zeek."

Zach, Zachary mouthed.

"Next time bring me some Twinkies."

"I will," Zachary lied.

"Wonder if the pieces are still there, in Hangar 18?" Robert's throat worked and he looked at the glass of water in Zachary's hand. "I can see the ones I shot like it was yesterday, those aliens. Hear the screams still. They didn't walk quite right, out in that farm field. Maybe it was because they were warming up, being outside of the refrigeration trailer, the heat bothering them. Maybe they were hurt so bad that they couldn't stand wholly upright. They had this jerky shuffle, arms loaded down with some gadgets they must have repaired. Walking like Frankenstein in an old black and white movie. That was what they shot us with, gadgets, ray guns. Green lighting, didn't I tell you? Can't blame them. They were fighting for their lives. I felt so awful killing them. It stuck in my craw for years."

"Maybe you'll forget it all again, Grandpa."

Robert shook his head. "I'm in Room 18 now, Zeek. I won't forget ever again. Three sixes."

"The devil's number."

"Won't be getting any of it out of my head now. No matter what this illness does to me. I'll probably forget everything else. Your name, Zeek. Can't remember the name of that little Mexican nurse." He reached a hand out for the glass of water. "But I'll set things right when the *Plain Dealer* reporter comes tomorrow. I'm going to tell him what I done, killing those aliens. Self defense, maybe. But I killed 'em nonetheless. The public should know about Roswell. That it's all real. Never was no weather balloon."

Zachary reluctantly relinquished the glass to the old man. "Drink up, Grandpa."

"Coming clean, Zeek, about all of this. I will clean my soul of the devil's handiwork."

"Eighteen," Zachary said. He stood and brushed his palms against his slacks.

"Eighteen. Three sixes." Robert downed the water in one long swallow. "You should come back tomorrow, Zeek, when the reporter is here. Maybe he'll take your picture, too. Maybe I'll have found that piece of the spaceship. Bet it's in that shoebox in my closet."

"I'll be back tomorrow, Grandpa," Zachary said. He walked down the steps and toward the parking lot without looking back. The drugs he'd slipped into the old man's water would take effect soon enough, ending the threat of publicity. Robert was so old, they wouldn't conduct an autopsy. The Army and the Air Force couldn't take the chance that someone might actually listen to the old man.

Tomorrow, Zach would come back one last time—to formally identify the body. He really was Robert's grandson, after all, and he did love the old coot—though not as much as he loved the U.S. of A. Yes, he'd come back and pay his respects, one last time, and pick up his inheritance—that shoebox from Room 18.

ROSWELL
Part II: The Cover-Up
by Nick Redfern

In the spring of 1993, the late Congressman Steven Schiff began to make inquiries with the Defense Department in an attempt to determine the truth surrounding certain aspects of the controversy. In an 11 March 1993 letter to the then Secretary of Defense, Les Aspin, Schiff wrote:

"Last fall I became aware of a strange series of events beginning in New Mexico over 45 years ago and involving personnel of what was then the Army Air Force. I have since reviewed the facts in some detail, and I am writing to request your assistance in arriving at a definitive explanation of what transpired and why.

"The inconsistency between repeated official denials and the public record and testimony of those involved has led to a great deal of sensational speculation and called into question the credibility of the Departments of Defense, Army, and the Air Force... "Therefore, Mr. Secretary, I respectfully request that you direct such a review be undertaken on a priority basis and that a representative or representatives of the Department of Defense and the responsible Military Departments promptly arrange to brief and provide me with a written report providing a current, complete, and detailed description and explanation of both the nature of what was recovered and all official actions taken on the matter..."

On 31 March 1993, and as a direct result of this action, Schiff received the following reply - not from Aspin but from Colonel Larry G. Shockley, USAF, Director, Plans and Operations: "I have received your letter of March 11, requesting information on alleged events which occurred in Roswell, New Mexico. In order to be of service to you, I have referred this matter to the National Archives and Records Administration for direct reply to you. If I can be of further assistance to you, please do not hesitate to let me know."

Schiff's office duly followed this on 7 April 1993 with a submission of material to Rudy deLeon, Special Assistant, Office of the Secretary of Defense, who replied:

"This is in regard to your recent letter to Secretary Aspin regarding alleged events which occurred in Roswell, New Mexico, in 1947.I, too, find these unexplained occurrences of great interest; however, these records are too old to be available here at the Pentagon. I would, therefore, recommend that you contact the National Archives for additional information, as I believe Colonel Shockley has already done on your behalf. I regret that my response in not more favorable, but I trust you will find this information helpful."

Once again, Congressman Schiff's office quickly sent a follow up letter to Secretary of Defense Aspin: "I realize that, after almost 46 years, it is a virtual certainty that all or most of the records concerning this incident have been archived. However, my staff and several independent investigators have conclusively established they are not in any of the unclassified, including previously classified, holdings of the National Archives. Moreover, it is my understanding that it is highly unlikely they reside in any of the classified files in the custody of the Archives.

"Wherever the documents may be, what is at issue is my request for a personal briefing and a written report on a matter involving actions taken by officials of the U.S. Army and U.S. Air Force, agencies under your purview. I realize the research required to uncover the relevant documents and related materials will take time and considerable effort, and I am prepared to wait a reasonable amount of time for this to be accomplished. However I expect the job to be done and my request to be addressed as set forth in the penultimate paragraph of my March letter..."

On 20 May 1993, Congressman Schiff received his reply from the National Archives:

"This is in reply to your letter of March 11, 1993, concerning information about a UFO sighting at Roswell, New Mexico, in 1947. The Department of the Air Force forwarded your letter, and we received it on May 6, 1993. The U.S. Air Force has retired to our custody its records on Project BLUE BOOK relating to the investigations of unidentified flying objects. Project BLUE BOOK has been declassified and the records are available for examination in our research room. The project closed in 1969 and we have no information after that date. We have received numerous requests concerning records relating to the Roswell incident among these records. We have not located any documentation relating to this event in Project BLUE BOOK records, or in any other pertinent Defense Department records in our custody."

Interpreting the fact that he was being passed back and forth from the Defense Department to the National Archives as stonewalling, Schiff once again determined to resolve the matter once and for all with Secretary Aspin:

"...While I realize that the Department of Defense, and you, Mr. Secretary, have been very busy in areas throughout the world, while also concerned with proposed changes in policy within the Department, I must insist on the courtesy of a reply to my letter, which is now three months old. To reiterate, while I am prepared to wait a reasonable length of time for the briefing I requested, I do insist that the Department do the research on my inquiry and report the findings to me. I also must insist on having my letters to the Department of Defense acknowledged and acted upon. I look forward to your response to my letters, and to the scheduled briefing. I will expect a reply to this inquiry by September 7th."

Nevertheless things did not go according to Schiff's wishes, and as a result, he contacted the General Accounting Office (the investigative arm of Congress) in a concerted effort to bring the Roswell controversy to rest, once and for all - as the *Washington Post* noted in January 1994:

"…GAO spokeswoman Laura A. Kopelson said the office's investigation stemmed from a meeting in October between Schiff and GAO Controller General Charles A Bowsher. Schiff complained then that the Defense Department had been 'unresponsive' to his inquiries about the 1947 incident…'I was getting pretty upset at all the running around,' Schiff said, adding that at his meeting with GAO officials, 'they made an offer to help.'… 'Generally, I'm a skeptic on UFOs and alien beings, but there are indications from the runaround that I got that whatever it was, it wasn't a balloon. Apparently, it's another government cover-up,' Schiff said. He called the Defense Department's lack of response 'astounding,' and said government accountability was an issue 'even larger than UFOs.'…He added, 'If the Defense Department had been responsive, it wouldn't have come to this.'" (1)

As a result of Schiff's efforts, the GAO duly launched an investigation and on 28 July 1995, a report surfaced from its National Security and International Affairs Division that disclosed the results of that same investigation. Commenting on an Air Force report on Roswell published in July 1994 (that preempted the GAO's report and that will be discussed shortly), the GAO informed Schiff that while it now seemed unlikely that the weather balloon explanation was correct after all, the Air Force had come to yet *another* conclusion in its attempt to lay the mystery of Roswell to rest:

"DOD informed us that the U.S. Air Force report of July 1994, entitled *Report of Air Force Research Regarding the Roswell Incident*, represents the extent of DOD records or information concerning the Roswell crash. The Air Force report concluded that there was no dispute that something happened near Roswell in July 1947 and that all available official materials indicated the most likely source of the wreckage recovered was one of the project MOGUL balloon trains. At the time of the Roswell crash, project MOGUL was a highly classified U.S. effort to determine the state of Soviet nuclear weapons research using balloons that carried radar reflectors and acoustic sensors."

And there was a genuinely intriguing surprise in store for GAO investigators when they began to search for records in an effort to try and better understand what had taken place: the *entire* outgoing messages from Roswell Army Air Field generated between October 1946 and December 1949 had been destroyed - under circumstances that could not be full determined, no less. As evidence of this, consider the following extract from the GAO report:

"In addition to unit history reports, we also searched for other government records on the Roswell crash. In this regard, the Chief Archivist for the National Personnel Records Center provided us with documentation indicating that (1) RAAF records such as finance and accounting, supplies, buildings and grounds, and other general administrative matters from March 1945 through December 1949 and (2) RAAF outgoing messages from October 1946 through December 1949 were destroyed. According to this official, the document disposition form did not properly indicate the authority under which the disposal action was taken. The Center's Chief Archivist stated that from his personal experience, many of the Air Force organizational records covering this time period were destroyed without entering a citation for the governing disposition authority. Our review of records control forms showing the destruction of other records—including outgoing RAAF messages for 1950—supports the Chief Archivist's viewpoint."

In essence, that details the GAO report on Roswell. And while the investigation certainly did not uncover any truly smoking guns or firmly resolve the Roswell affair to everyone's satisfaction (if anything, the inexplicably missing RAAF files of 1946-9 only intensified the debate), it did at least prompt the Air Force to present its *third* explanation for what occurred at Roswell – the crash landing of a highly secret Project Mogul balloon train. For his part, however, Congressman Schiff (who described the GAO report as "professional, conscientious and thorough") remained troubled by the apparent disappearance of years of outgoing documentation from Roswell Army Air Field:

"It is my understanding that these outgoing messages were permanent records, which should never have been destroyed. The GAO could not identify who destroyed the messages, or why." And as he added: "At least this effort caused the Air Force to acknowledge that the crashed vehicle was no weather balloon. That explanation never fit the fact of high military security used at the time." **(2)**

The Air Force was unmoved, however. In the Executive Summary of the Air Force's July 1994 *Report of Air Force Research Regarding the Roswell Incident*, its author, Colonel Richard L. Weaver, USAF, Director, Security and Special Program Oversight, wrote:

"Records were located and thoroughly explored concerning a then-TOP SECRET balloon project, designed to attempt to monitor Soviet nuclear tests, known as Project Mogul. Additionally, several surviving project personnel were located and interviewed, as was the only surviving person who recovered debris from the original Roswell site in 1947... Comparison of all information developed or obtained indicated that the material recovered near Roswell was consistent with a balloon device and most likely from one of the Mogul balloons that had not been previously recovered." **(3)**

While Colonel Weaver's report delved deeply into the world of Project Mogul, most noticeable by its stark absence was any serious attempt to address the statements of those sources that claimed to have seen unusual bodies at the Roswell site. Indeed, this aspect of the controversy received only the following, brief statement from Weaver: "It should also be noted here that there was little mentioned in this report about the recovery of the so-called 'alien bodies.' [T]he recovered wreckage was from a Project Mogul balloon. There were no 'alien' passengers therein." (4)

Three years after Colonel Weaver's report was published, however, the Air Force made a surprising acknowledgement that the reported sightings of strange bodies at Roswell *did* have a basis in fact. Not only that: so compelled by then was the Air Force to address the "bodies" issue that it authorized the release of yet *another* report on Roswell. The final word was apparently not the final word, after all.

Entitled *The Roswell Report: Case Closed*, the Air Force's latest report on the New Mexico events of 1947 was published in 1997 and marked the 50th anniversary of the incident at Roswell. The report did little to dampen the notoriety surrounding the case, however. Indeed, the question of *why* the Air Force had concluded that there was a pressing need on its part to explain the reports of unusual bodies found in New Mexico (when it could have summarily dismissed them as hoaxes or modern-day folklore), arguably only heightened the interest in what did or did not occur.

Written by Captain James McAndrew (an Intelligence Applications Officer assigned to the Secretary of the Air Force Declassification and Review Team at the Pentagon who had served special tours of duty with the Drug Enforcement Administration), the report focused practically all of its 231 pages on the alleged recovery of the strange bodies and asserted that:

"'Aliens' observed in the New Mexico desert were probably anthropomorphic test dummies that were carried aloft by U.S. Air Force high altitude balloons for scientific research. The 'unusual' military activities in the New Mexico desert were high altitude research balloon launch and recovery operations. The reports of military units that always seemed to arrive shortly after the crash of a flying saucer to retrieve the saucer and 'crew,' were actually accurate descriptions of Air Force personnel engaged in anthropomorphic dummy recovery operations."

There is no doubt (indeed, it is a matter of historical record) that the Air Force conducted a wide array of tests using crash test dummies in New Mexico and that at least some of these tests *did* occur in the vicinities of both the White Sands Proving Ground and the town of Roswell. But were those same tests responsible – either in part or in whole – for the stories concerning highly unusual-looking bodies recovered by the military during the summer of 1947?

Declassified documentation made available by the Air Force shows that forty-three high-altitude balloon flights carrying 67 anthropomorphic dummies (that were transported to heights of up to 98,000 feet) were launched and recovered throughout New Mexico. And as *The Roswell Report: Case Closed* notes: "Due to prevailing wind conditions, operational factors and ruggedness of the terrain, the majority of dummies impacted outside the confines of military reservations in eastern New Mexico, near Roswell, and in areas surrounding the Tularosa Valley in south central New Mexico."

For the majority of the tests, dummies were flown to altitudes between 30,000 and 98,000 feet attached to a specially designed rack suspended below a high altitude balloon; and on several flights, the dummies were mounted in the door of an experimental, high-altitude balloon gondola. Upon reaching the desired altitude, the dummies would be released and "free-fell" for several minutes before deployment of the main parachute.

Dummies utilized in these operations were typically outfitted with standard equipment, including a one-piece flight suit, olive drab or gray in color, and a parachute pack. In addition, the dummies were fitted with an instrumentation kit that contained accelerometers, pressure transducers, and a camera to record movements of the dummy during free-fall.

The recovery of the dummies was handled by Holloman Air Force Base's Balloon Branch; and under normal circumstances, eight to twelve civilian and military recovery personnel would secure the landing site of one or more of the dummies, and would be complemented by a variety of aircraft and vehicles, including a wrecker, a six-by-six, a weapons carrier, and L-20 observation and C-47 transport aircraft. On one occasion southwest of Roswell, Lieutenant Raymond A. Madson even conducted a search for dummies on horseback.

Documentation reviewed by the Air Force as part of its attempt to lay to rest the claims that strange corpses were recovered from the New Mexico desert in the summer of 1947, demonstrated that Holloman Air Force Base, New Mexico, has – to date - launched and recovered no less than 2,500 high altitude balloons, with the majority having been launched by the Holloman Balloon Branch. But under what circumstances did these operations begin?

In 1946, as a result of research conducted for Project Mogul, Charles B. Moore, the New York University graduate student working under contract for the Army Air Forces, made a significant technological discovery concerning the use of polythene for high altitude balloon construction. Polythene, a lightweight plastic that can withstand stresses of a high altitude environment differed drastically from, and greatly exceeded, the capabilities of standard rubber weather balloons used previously. As an example of this, polythene balloons flown by the Air Force have reached recorded altitudes of 170,000 feet and lifted payloads of 15,000 pounds.

It is also a fact that in the late 1940s, a characteristic associated with the large – and newly invented – polythene balloons, was that they were often misidentified as flying saucers. In fact, according to Bernard D. Gildenberg, Balloon Branch Meteorologist and Engineer, so many flying saucer reports were generated as a result of the balloons launched from Holloman AFB that accounts from police and news services were regularly used by Holloman's technicians to supplement early balloon-tracking techniques.

Indeed, balloons launched at Holloman AFB in 1947 generated an especially high number of flying saucer reports due to the excellent visibility in the New Mexico region. Also, the balloons, flown at altitudes of approximately 100,000 feet, were illuminated before the earth during the periods just after sunset and just before sunrise. In this instance, receiving sunlight before the earth, the plastic balloons appeared as large bright objects against a dark sky. Also, with the refractive and translucent qualities of polythene, the balloons appeared to change color, size and shape.

Research also undertaken by the Air Force as a part of its Roswell investigation showed that one of the key areas of investigation in New Mexico at the time that involved balloon-based studies was in relation to "space biology" and the way in which cosmic ray particles might adversely affect living tissue; while other projects gathered meteorological data and collected air samples to determine the composition of the atmosphere.

The Air Force's new research also led it to elaborate further upon the strange debris recovered by rancher Brazel on the Foster Ranch: "As early as May 1948, polythene balloons coated or laminated with aluminum were flown from Holloman AFB and the surrounding area. Beginning in August 1955, large numbers of these balloons were flown as targets in the development of radar guided air-to-air missiles. Various accounts of the 'Roswell Incident' often described thin, metal-like materials that when wadded into a ball, returned to their original shape. These accounts are consistent with the properties of polythene balloons laminated with aluminum. These balloons were typically launched from points west of the White Sands Proving Ground, floated over the range as targets, and descended in the areas northeast of White Sands Proving Ground where the 'strange' materials were allegedly found."

With the reports of strange bodies recovered near Roswell relegated to the world of the crash test dummy, the Air Force then focused its attention upon the claims (many of which surfaced from Roswell mortician W. Glenn Dennis) that alien bodies were taken to the base hospital at Roswell Army Air Field following the events of the summer of 1947.

The relevant section of *The Roswell Report: Case Closed* runs to no less than 50 pages and I would urge anyone with an interest in the case to review it in depth. For the sake of space, however, I cite the Air Force's conclusions on this particular aspect of the affair: "Claims of bodies at the Roswell Army Air Field hospital were most likely a combination of two separate incidents," asserted the Air Force.

The former incident occurred on 26 June, 1956, when an Air Force refueling plane caught fire while in flight and crashed, killing all eleven crew members. The corpses of the crewmen were soaked through with fuel and burned beyond recognition, and some even lost numerous body parts. Some autopsies of the victims were conducted at civilian facilities, and McAndrew's report suggests that this incident was the source of the claim that the military had retrieved gruesome, alien bodies that were described as "black" and "very mangled" by witnesses.

The second incident that the Air Force believed led rise to the claims that alien bodies were transported to the base hospital occurred on 21 May, 1959, when Air Force Captain Dan Fulgham suffered a serious head injury when the balloon he was piloting crash landed in New Mexico. His head, severely swollen with blood, was described by one associate as "just a big blob," and McAndrew suggested that Fulgham's condition may have caused a civilian observer at Walker Air Force Base hospital to later report seeing an "alien creature" enter the facility. (5)

At the time of its release, the conclusions of the Air Force's (final?) report provoked a furor of controversy – for two key reasons. While there is absolutely no doubt that tests utilizing anthropomorphic dummies *were* widespread in New Mexico *and* in the Roswell region, the Air Force's report largely and very carefully glosses over the fact that these particular tests did not begin until the early 1950s. Likewise, the two events that the Air Force asserted led to the legends of alien bodies taken to the Roswell Army Air Field hospital occurred in the *late* 1950s and long after the purported incident of 1947.

Indeed, this was an issue not lost on the media during the Air Force's press conference at the Pentagon that accompanied the release of the report in July 1997. When asked by a reporter, "How do you square the UFO enthusiasts saying that they're talking about 1947, and you're talking about dummies used in the 50's, almost a decade later?" Air Force spokesman, Colonel John Haynes replied: "Well, I'm afraid that's a problem that we have with time compression. I don't know what they saw in '47, but I'm quite sure it probably was Project Mogul. But I think if you find that people talk about things over a period of time, they begin to lose exactly when the date was." **(6)**

Notably, too, in the wake of the report's release, Associated Press revealed that no less a source than the project officer at Holloman Air Force Base, Lt. Colonel Raymond A. Madson, (Ret.) wasn't "buying" the latest Air Force explanation of what occurred in Roswell in July 1947 – despite the fact that Madson was cited in the report prepared by the Air Force. **(7)** Neither was Stanton Friedman:

"One of the silliest official USAF stories is the crash test dummy nonsense. I spoke in person with Colonel Madson, whose picture is in the *Case Closed* volume and was heavily involved in the research program. He is adamant that the explanation doesn't fit. Remember that the dummies had to be the same height and weight as air force pilots. None were dropped anywhere near the two crash sites and none were dropped earlier than 6 years *after* the 1947 events." **(8)**

And according to Walter Haut, the man who issued the original press release from Roswell Army Air Field in July 1947:

"It's just to me another cover-up. If you're dropping a dummy, any dummy would know what a dummy looks like." **(9)**

In essence, the material related in the above two chapters represents the current state of play with regard to the Roswell controversy. The Air Force stands firmly behind its Mogul and crash test dummy explanations, UFO proponents assert that this is all part of a huge and on-going conspiracy designed to hide the fact that an alien spacecraft crashed at Roswell, and the general public and the media look on with a mixture of interest, puzzlement, bemusement and amusement.

As time inexorably passes by, and those implicated in the Roswell affair pass on due to the inevitability of old age, the chances of us getting to the bottom of the mystery of what really occurred at Roswell back in the summer of 1947 get slimmer every year. But of two things we can be certain: (a) something decidedly strange happened on that fateful July 1947 day; and (b) more than sixty years later, the Air Force's seemingly-ever-changing and mutating explanations cast considerable doubt on the idea that the world's most famous UFO incident was due to nothing more than conventional balloons and crash-test-dummies.

References:
1. *Washington Post*, 14 January 1994.
2. *Results of a Search for Records Concerning the 1947 Crash Near Roswell, New Mexico*, General Accounting Office, 28 July 1995.
3. *Report of Air Force Research Regarding the Roswell Incident*, Colonel Richard L. Weaver, United States Air Force, 1994. *The Roswell Report: Fact Vs. Fiction in the New Mexico Desert*, Colonel Richard L. Weaver, United States Air Force, 1995.
4. Ibid.
5. *The Roswell Report: Case Closed*, Captain James McAndrew, United States Air Force, 1997.
6. Press Conference, Pentagon.
7. *Associated Press*, 5 July 1997
8. *Scientist Challenges Air Force Regarding UFOs*, www.v-j-enterprises.com/sfchlgaf.html
9. www.moreabcnews.go.com/dispatches/bureaus/roswell702/roswell702.html

LAST CALL AT CORONA
by Stephen D. Sullivan

It's nearly three A.M. and I'm sitting in my room at the Desert View Motel, twenty miles southeast of Corona, New Mexico, waiting for the aliens to arrive.

I never believed in aliens—until tonight. I once worked with a writer who said his dog had been eaten by a monster from outer space, but I assumed he was lying. Authors are professional liars anyway, and a smart freelance photographer learns to take everything his feature writer tells him with a grain of salt. Believing the bull that authors sling around can lead you into a lot of trouble.

The same goes for believing strange women who appear half-dressed on the doorstep of your motel room in the middle of the night. Sucker that I am, I had let her come inside anyway . . .

"Hi," the woman at the door said, flashing a hopeful smile. She was about five-foot-two and dressed in a pink tube top and very brief blue-jean shorts. A wavy blonde mane framed her heart-shaped face and tumbled across her bare shoulders. Her hair was wet, and tiny beads of water trickled down her tanned skin; she must have just stepped out of the shower, because there hadn't been any rain in this part of New Mexico for weeks—maybe longer. "I'm Beth."

I stood in the doorway with my hands propped on either side of the frame, blocking her access to my room, as I peered past "Beth" into the desert night. I half expected to find a muscular pimp hiding in the darkness. I'd nearly fallen victim to a similar come-along while photographing Aztec ruins near Mexico City, and I didn't want to stumble into that trap again. Despite my

68

trepidation, I didn't see anyone lurking in the dusty motel parking lot, waiting to jump me.

"I'm Tom," I replied. "I don't remember ordering room service. Hell, I didn't even know this joint had any."

"I'm not with the motel," she said. "I'm a guest, like you. Is that your beat-up jeep in the parking lot? The one with the Seattle plates?"

"Maybe."

Her blue eyes flashed attractively in the light spilling out from inside my room. "'Cause if it is, I need a favor."

"How big a favor?" I asked.

She leaned forward, craning her neck to look inside my room, while, at the same time, giving me an unavoidable view of her bosom. The points in her tube top indicated she was cold; not surprising as the desert temperature had dropped thirty degrees since dusk. "Aren't you going to ask me in?" she replied.

Now, I'm familiar with scantily clad women in both my capacity an eligible bachelor and as a freelance photographer, and usually there's nothing I like better than some nymph wanting to get into my motel room. But something about Beth was making my "spider-sense" tingle. Unfortunately, before that sensible caution could make its way to my forebrain, I found my lips saying, "Sure. Come on in."

I dropped my arms from the doorframe to admit her, and silently cursed myself for thinking below the belt—as usual.

"Thanks," she said, brushing tantalizingly up against me as she sidled past. The damp scent of jasmine in her hair lingered in my nostrils as I followed her in.

She plopped herself down into the room's sole chair, a padded vinyl and tube-steel abomination that had somehow escaped unscathed from the 1960s. The chair squeaked loudly despite the fact that Beth couldn't have weighed more than one-hundred pounds soaking wet.

"Can I get you a bottle of water?" I asked. "Sorry I don't have anything more, but I usually travel light."

"I've got some beer in my room," she offered. "I could fetch a couple if you like."

"Maybe later," I replied. Sharing beers with a cute girl was always a great way to end the day, but the cautious portions of me were now in better control. Those parts knew that strange women seldom arrived unannounced in your room after eleven P.M. just to offer you a beer. "You said you needed a favor?"

She settled into the chair and crossed her long, tanned legs. Dad always told me good things come in small packages, and despite my being exhausted after finishing my assignment and driving up from Carlsbad, she was looking mighty good. I sat down on the bed opposite her; it squeaked, too, though not as much as the chair.

"My Land Rover broke down," Beth said. "You probably saw it in front of room six when you drove in." I nodded—it had been the only other car in the lot aside from the one next to the office—and she continued. "The thing is . . . there's somewhere I need to be tonight."

My bed? the less-sensible part of me wanted to reply, but, instead, I went with, "Where?"

"A spot in the desert a couple of miles from here," she said. "It's too far to walk, or I'd just hike out there myself."

She definitely didn't look like she was dressed for a hike. "So, you want me to. . . ?"

"Loan me your jeep," she said. "I can pay for it." When she noticed my skepticism, she added, "I'm an investigator—doing research."

"In the desert, in the middle of the night."

"Yes."

"Why not just rent a car?"

"All the rental places are closed for the weekend, and the motel manager got called away—some kind of family emergency—so I can't ask her, either."

And probably, the manager wouldn't respond to your considerable charms the way I am, I thought. "Look," I said, "I don't know what kind of scam you're trying to pull here, Beth, or what kind of deal you're looking to score tonight. And—You know what?—I have no intention of finding out. It's been a long day amid a long week, and I've worked very hard, and I'm tired, and I've still got a long way to drive before I get home to Seattle. So, sorry, though I like the package, I'm not buying whatever it is you're selling. Maybe some other time." I stood, walked to the door, and held it open.

She didn't budge from the ugly vinyl chair. "Tom, you're my only hope," she pleaded. "I'd throw myself at you but, frankly, I'm just not that kind of girl."

Could have fooled me, I thought.

She must have noticed my eyes wandering over what little there was of her outfit. "Okay," she said, "I admit I did sexy myself up a bit before I came over to see you, but that's only because I need this so desperately. If I don't get out into the desert in the next two hours, I'll miss *them*, and it may be ages before I'll get another chance."

"Them what?" I asked, immediately regretting it.

"The aliens."

Gorgeous and sopping wet or not, I'd had as much of her as I could take. "Okay," I said, "that's it, Beth, or whatever your name is. You need to get out of my room now, before I call the manager."

"She's gone for the night, remember?"

I swore. "Okay, I'll call the cops, then," I said. "There has to be some kind of authority even in this Godforsaken place."

My threat didn't rattle her at all. "Nearest cop is twenty miles away in Corona," she observed. "It'll take them a good long while to get here. I'm sure that before they arrive, you and I can work something out."

I closed the door again. "I thought you just told me you're *not* that kind of girl."

"Well, I'm not, but you're a photographer, right?" She nodded toward my camera bag and some other equipment that I'd stowed in one corner of the room.

"So, what? You're going to pose for me?"

"Nope," she said. "I'm going to get you a picture that will make you famous. You've heard of the Roswell crash?"

"Sure. I passed through Roswell on the way here. Great bloody tourist trap."

"You bet. But did you know that the Roswell crash wasn't actually in Roswell? It really happened on a ranch just a couple of miles from here. The incident just became known as the 'Roswell crash' because there's an air base there, and that's where the crash investigators came from."

She took a deep breath, which made those the twin points in her top stand out even more. "Suppose I could get you a picture of the aliens that crashed in Roswell."

I looked doubtful. "So . . . what? You know where the bodies are buried? That crash was over fifty years ago."

"Sure, but the aliens are coming back tonight," she said. "And when they do, you and I are going to be there."

I leaned up against the door jamb. "Look, Beth, I'm sure you're a very nice girl, and you certainly have enthusiasm on your side, but I don't believe in aliens. And furthermore, even if I did believe in them, why should I believe that you've got some secret information that's going to allow me to get pictures?"

"Because I've got three hundred bucks that says you'll drive me out into the desert and play along for the next couple of hours."

"There isn't any room in your outfit for a wallet," I noted.

"I don't have the money on me, but I've got it, and if you agree to drive me into the desert, I'll give it to you. In advance."

"And if that's still not enough?" I asked.

She smiled. "Well . . . then maybe I *am* that kind of girl—or I *will be* after I get what I want. But the only way you're going to find out is by rolling the dice, taking my money, and going for a ride with me.

"So, what's it gonna be? You gonna drive me into the desert, make three hundred dollars, and maybe get lucky, or are you going to turn me down, sit in this room awake all night, and play, 'Woulda, coulda, shoulda' with yourself?"

Every cell in my brain was telling me to turn her down.

She got the money from her motel room, and I called my editor Shelly and left a voice mail, just so someone would know where to look for the body in case I didn't come back.

When Beth returned, I was more than mildly disappointed to discover that she'd changed out of her scanties and into something resembling Indiana Jones' summer wear: khaki shirt and shorts, tall socks, and hiking boots. The only concession to my libido was that she'd tied the shirt off above her waist, exposing her tanned midriff. *At least*, I thought, *she isn't sporting a tinfoil hat*.

"Is that what you're wearing?" she asked, glancing at my t-shirt, shorts, and sandals.

"I thought we were driving," I said.

"We're driving *most* of the way," she replied. "But we'll have to do a little hiking, too. Of course, you *might* be all right. Most of the snakes and scorpions sleep at night."

"I'll change and meet you at the jeep," I said.

Ten minutes later we had turned south off of Route 247 and were bouncing over the trackless New Mexican desert, following coordinates displayed on Beth's GPS unit. The dusty terrain was growing progressively rougher, though my jeep—a vintage army model—was well up to the trek. There was no moon, but billions of stars blazed brightly overhead, illuminating the landscape with a dull bluish glow. The jeep's headlights cut a brilliant yellow-white swath through the starlit scenery: low hills, rocks, and greasewood punctuated by the occasional jackrabbit or coyote.

"So, we're going to the original Roswell crash site?" I asked as I drove.

She gave me a quizzical look. "What good would that do?"

"I thought maybe the aliens were coming back to pick up survivors . . . or something."

"Have you ever heard of a UFO landing twice in the same place?" she asked.

"I guess if they did there'd be better evidence that they actually exist," I replied.

"You bet," she said. "But you're forgetting that the 'Roswell' UFO *crashed*. It actually meant to land somewhere else."

"So that's where we're going?"

Beth looked at me the way one might an underachieving student. "No. Finding alien landing zones is much more complicated than that," she said. "The group I belong to has done a lot of research, and we've figured out the probable landing site of the 1947 UFO."

"Group?" I asked.

"PSI-ET: the Paranormal & Supernatural Investigation - Expedition Team. We have over three hundred and twenty members."

I didn't know what to say, so I kept my mouth shut.

She continued. "We believe that saucer sightings are related to both astronomical conjunctions and fluctuations in the earth's magnetic field. Those fluctuations cause the convergence of what are commonly known as 'ley lines,' which is what attracts the UFOs."

"I thought 'ley lines' were invisible supernatural highways or something. They're supposed to connect places like Stonehenge with other ancient monuments. Aren't they?"

She gave me an indulgent "you're not as dumb as you look" smile. "They do, but the charted lines aren't as stable as most people assume. What PSI-ET discovered is that there are fluctuations in the permanent lines over time. Changes in the Earth's magnetic field can create temporary lines, and those lines sometimes pull the known lines off course. With the right magnetic fluctuations, lines can converge, and that's what UFOs are attracted to. That's what's happening tonight."

I was about to say, *Why in hell would anyone believe a crock of pseudo-scientific babble like that?* But just at that moment, the jeep crested a bump that bounced both of us toward the ceiling, so that all that came out of my mouth was, "Why. . . ?"

She frowned. "We don't know. Maybe the aliens are interested in the earth's magnetosphere. Or maybe they need the energy to refuel or something. When we see them tonight, maybe we can ask them."

I would have laughed, but the way she said, *"When we see them tonight,"* was so earnest that I kept my mouth shut. Laughing at a pretty girl—even a slightly crazy one—is seldom a good way to eventually lure her into bed.

"If tonight's convergence is such a big deal," I asked, "why isn't the whole group out here with you? Don't they want to see the aliens?"

Even in the dim light from the GPS, I could see her pained expression. "I . . . we had a . . . disagreement," Beth said. "Some of the people in my local PSI-ET group didn't think my calculations were right."

"That would be locally here—in New Mexico?"

"No. Back home in Frosthaven, Wisconsin."

"I knew a writer from Frosthaven once," I said. Curiously enough, that writer insisted his dog had been eaten by aliens. "That's a long way from here."

"Thus, my dead Land Rover," she said with a shrug. "At least it got me this far. Hey, slow down, we're almost there."

I scanned the cones of pale light in front of the jeep, but nothing looked different, just more scrub and sand and rock, though we'd grown considerably closer to a line of rugged hills to the south.

Beth checked her GPS unit. "The spot we're looking for is just over that ridge ahead," she said, pointing.

The ridge she indicated looked more like an escarpment to me. "No way the jeep's getting over that," I told her.

"Then we'll just have to go on foot," she replied.

"Of course we will," I said. *In for an inch, in for a foot, I guess.*

"Pull over here," she said, indicating a random spot next to the precipitous, rocky hillside.

I skidded the jeep to a halt beside a scraggly yucca. Beth hopped out, peering intently at her GPS, and I followed.

"Aren't you going to bring your camera?" she asked.

Naturally, I hadn't considered it. Why bring a camera on a snipe hunt? "Yeah, of course," I said. "I just got swept up in the moment."

"We have to keep our heads clear," she cautioned. "This is going to be the most important night of our lives."

Again, I almost laughed, but covered myself by opening the back of the jeep and loudly hauling out my SLR. "Didn't you bring a camera of your own?"

"Sure. But my equipment isn't as good as yours; it's only a handheld."

I watched that fat pitch flash right over the plate without swinging for the fence.

"Do you have an infrared flash and film?" she asked.

"Sorry. Camera's digital."

"Don't you need IR for night shots?"

"Nope," I said. "Slow speed and/or a fill flash always does the trick."

"Darn." She turned and headed toward the stony ridge, crunching over the dry ground. "You'll just have to make do with what you have," she called back to me. "Try to use available light, if you can."

"Do you think there will be any?" I asked, shouldering my camera bag and hurrying to catch up.

"UFOs are often luminous," she replied. "You should be able to pick up something."

I remembered all the smeared glowing orbs and fuzzy pie-plate photos I'd seen on TV that were supposed to be UFOs, and while I knew I could definitely do something that rotten, my professional pride demanded more.

"I thought we were going for Pulitzer material here," I said.

She turned and flashed a rousing smile. "You bet," she said. "But first we have to make sure they're friendly."

"How are we going to do that?"

"I guess I'll just have to walk up to them and ask," she replied without a trace of irony.

"So, should I take the picture before, after, or during your disintegration?"

"That's very nineteen-fifties thinking, Mister . . ." She stopped in her tracks and looked at me. "You know, Tom, I never did ask your last name."

I grinned, trying not to look too wolfish. "I don't know your last name, either, Beth. I thought this was going to be one of those anonymous UFO hookups."

She extended her hand and I shook it. "Rhule. Beth Rhule."

Her fingers were warm and smooth. "Tom Henderson."

"Pleased to meet you, Tom Henderson. Thanks for helping me out."

"You're welcome," I said, still hoping that I'd get something out of the evening's hike besides three-hundred dollars and aching feet. She began climbing, and I admired her ass by starlight as she went ahead of me.

We crested the escarpment and looked into the arroyo beyond. It was a barren pocket, perhaps a hundred feet across and three times that long, tucked into the rocky hills. The bottom of the narrow bowl was flat and sandy, with few stones and only a handful of knee-high brownish tumbleweed marring its surface. By starlight, I saw no sign that either humans or animals had ever been in the arroyo before.

Planting herself atop the rocks like a climber at the summit of Everest, Beth checked her GPS and beamed. "We've found it!"

"I don't see any aliens here," I replied. In fact, I didn't see anything even remotely interesting—aside from Beth.

She checked her watch. "They're not here yet," she said, "but this is the spot, based on my calculations. We made good time." She shone her flashlight into the arroyo and began picking her way down the rocky hillside. Her boots kicked up small avalanches of gravel, which clattered to the hollow's floor.

I followed, holding my camera bag the way a protective mother cradles her newborn. No way did I want to damage several thousand dollars worth of equipment on this absurd outing. "How long are we going to wait?" I asked.

"It's half past midnight now," she said, "and the ley lines won't converge until one-eleven A.M." She stopped behind a wide smooth rock about twenty feet above the arroyo floor. "This should be a good spot to wait until they land."

"I thought you wanted to meet these aliens face-to-face," I said, settling in behind the rock next to her.

"I do," she said, "and we will. But I don't want to scare them away. They're shy about meeting people. That's one of the many reasons there's not better evidence of alien contact."

And here I thought it was because all supposed contactees had forgotten to take their medication. "Are you sure they'll be happy to see us once they're here?" I asked, fighting hard to remain serious.

She switched off her flashlight. "We'll find out soon enough."

Or not, I thought and settled in for a long, cold, boring wait.

I intended to give her until two A.M. or perhaps half-past before calling her bluff. After that, I figured I'd either convince her to either fool around or head back to the motel, or maybe both. Unfortunately, we never got that far.

I'd left my watch back at the hotel, but I could tell when we were getting close to eleven past one because, as time went on, Beth checked her watch more and more frequently. Each time she did, the look of concern on her pretty face grew more grave. During the final minutes, she started peering up into the sky, watching for the expected space ship.

But nothing happened.

"I . . . I *can't* have miscalculated!" she muttered, more to herself than to me.

I wanted to say something comforting, but—despite her starlit beauty—all that kept popping into my head were sarcastic quips like, *"Well, this was worth losing sleep over,"* or *"I'm glad I'm out here in the desert, freezing my ass off rather than snuggling down in my nice warm motel bed."*

Beth was so intent on stargazing, and I was so busy keeping my mouth shut, that we almost didn't notice when the air in the arroyo below began shimmering. The atmosphere wavered, like heat rising off of a paved road, despite the chilly night. Then, a faint glow, like shifting, iridescent mist, appeared above the parched earth.

I noticed the effect first, and gripped Beth's shoulder to alert her.

Her blue eyes went wide. "Get your camera out," she whispered.

Completely stunned that anything out-of-the-ordinary was happening at all, I fumbled with my camera bag. Despite my suddenly sweaty hands, I managed to pull out the big SLR and switch it on.

Beth leaned on the wide, smooth rock in front of us, peering over the top toward the anomaly below; I took up a position beside her. We were so close that I could feel the heat of her body next to mine, but for once, I had other things on my mind besides sex. What was happening in the arroyo was like nothing I'd ever seen before.

The air near the far side of the gulley shimmered more intensely, like ripples running outward from a big stone thrown into a pond. The soft glow continued to spread, and then, in the center of it, a shape suddenly formed.

It didn't just appear out of nothingness; rather, it seemed to push its way out of the ripples, like a diver emerging from deep water. This was no living being, though; it was a symmetrical, metallic shape—the proverbial flying saucer.

The object was about thirty feet across and shaped like a series of discs stacked atop each other: a small one on the bottom, then a larger one, then the largest in the middle, with two smaller ones, mirroring the bottom ones, on top—five tiers in all. It reminded me of the stepped pyramids of the Aztecs, but it showed no signs of human workmanship or markings of any kind.

"You see?" Beth hissed. She dug her fingernails into my left forearm so hard that I thought she'd draw blood. "I told you they'd come!"

I nodded, all erotic thoughts and smart-ass quips having fled from my brain.

"That was amazing!" she whispered. "They didn't come from the sky at all. Some people have theorized that UFOs come from other dimensions, and now we've seen the proof. We've seen one materialize!"

Again, I nodded dumbly.

"Take a picture!" she whispered.

My hands shaking, I positioned the camera atop the rock and squeezed the shutter.

For a moment, a burst of pure white light filled the arroyo, and I saw the image of the metallic saucer shape form on the camera's LCD. It wasn't the best picture I'd ever taken—not by a long shot; I took a deep breath to calm my nerves and prepared to shoot another.

"No flash!" Beth hissed urgently. "Turn off the flash! They'll see us! We don't want them to see us yet!"

Cursing beneath my breath, I fumbled with the settings and turned the flash off. As I did, the saucer itself began to glow.

Beth and I hunkered down further behind the rock, the thought of taking more pictures momentarily forgotten.

"Do you think they saw us?" I asked, immediately aware of how insane that sounded.

But this was clearly a crazy situation. Could she have drugged me sometime during the evening? It didn't seem possible. The only food and drink I'd consumed since meeting her were from my own supplies.

"I don't know," she replied. "Just wait, and keep your head down."

As if I needed her to tell me that. I kept the camera ready, though, and managed to squeeze off a few shots—without the flash—as the glow increased.

If these don't turn out, no one will ever believe me, I thought. *Hell, they probably won't believe me even if they do turn out!*

I checked the LCD to see how I was doing, but the shots looked fuzzy, probably because I couldn't stop my hands from shaking. But before I could seize complete control of my nerves, the saucer shape seemed to fold into itself, and a black, vertical slit opened in its middle.

The opening began as a tiny crack, but soon widened in the center until it resembled the ovoid pupil of a cat's eye.

Just as I thought, *That almost looks like a doorway,* the light around the saucer faded and something—or, rather, things—stepped out of the dark crevice.

There were three of them, all dressed in black, skin-tight suits. They resembled human beings, but shorter and thinner, with bulbous heads and bulging black eyes. They had iridescent grayish skin that looked slightly scaly, tiny mouths, and very little in the way of ears or noses.

Yeah, just like in the movies; you can imagine my surprise. Not only had Beth been right about the time and place of their appearance, the aliens also looked exactly like all the kooks said they did. Who'd have figured that?

Beth sat next to me, peering over the top of the rock, eyes wide and mouth agape; apparently she was just as shocked as I.

All three aliens—What else could I call them?—held small, box-like devices in their bony, three-fingered hands. I couldn't tell what the gadgets were, though they looked like something out of *Star Trek*. Communicators? Scanners? Weapons? Maybe all three.

I wasn't particularly anxious to find out, even though my newshound instincts had taken over, and I'd managed to squeeze off a few more shots, despite trembling hands. *Pulitzer Prize, here I come.*

The creatures swept the arroyo with their black eyes, though they didn't notice Beth or me. Then, two fanned out to either side, while the one in the middle stooped down and began scraping at the dirt with the instrument in its right hand. I noticed green streams of light, like laser beams, playing over the surrounding landscape. The lights emanated from the devices in the hands of the flanking aliens.

Were they scientists exploring our world? Did they create the rift between earth and wherever they came from, or were they just taking advantage of it? Had they tracked down the right time and place on their world like Beth had on ours? Or was this all part of some drugged-out hallucination? Could a man be unwittingly hypnotized by a tube top and a pair of tight shorts?

I turned toward Beth to make sure that she was seeing the same uncanny things I was, but she was gone.

For a moment, I felt relieved; people didn't disappear in real life, so I must be dreaming. That was it. Now it all made perfect sense. Then I spotted her walking downhill, and a chill enveloped my entire body.

While I'd been busy snapping pictures, Beth had stepped out from behind our sheltering rock and was ambling toward the aliens. She held her hands outstretched to the side in what she must have figured was a universal sign of peace and goodwill.

I barely had time to swear under my breath before they noticed her.

For an instant, all three aliens froze, the same way a lizard will freeze atop a rock when it spots a hawk circling high above. Then the one on the left swung its device toward her.

Green laser-light flashed across the ground in front of Beth and the air sizzled. A buzzing hum filled my ears, and the tang of ozone tainted the air. Smoke rose from the dirt where the light touched it, and a bit of sagebrush near her feet turned to ash.

Beth stopped dead in her tracks.

"I c-come in peace," she stammered. Under other circumstances, I would have groaned. Right at the moment, though, I was terrified for her life—and my own.

I expected the weapon-thing in the alien's hand to turn her into dust, but the green light didn't flash out again. Instead, all three aliens converged on her simultaneously, as though they were puppets being controlled by the same strings.

The two on the sides angled to surround her, while the one in the middle walked straight forward, raising the device in its hand.

"Friend," Beth said sincerely, though her voice still quavered.

The middle alien raised its gizmo to the height of Beth's head, and an array of blue-white lights flashed on the object's surface. The other two aliens closed in on her from either side.

Beth's blue eyes rolled upward and her knees wobbled; she looked about to faint. The aliens sprang forward, and so did I.

Skidding down the rock-covered slope, I reached the bottom just as the aliens were about to seize the swooning researcher. I flipped my camera's flash on, hit the auto-wind function, and fired off a quick succession of shots. The flash unit exploded in a dazzling series of bright, white bursts.

The aliens screamed, a kind of high, keening hiss. They covered their huge, lidless eyes and backed away just enough for me to bull through the group. I grabbed Beth around the waist and dragged her stumbling upslope.

"W-what. . . ?" she muttered.

"Keep moving," I urged, pushing her uphill in front of me.

I glanced back, but the aliens were only shadows moving at the edges of my vision. I heard the buzzing hum of the laser device and saw the green light playing over the rocks to our left. I don't know if the aliens were lousy shots, or maybe the gizmo wasn't really made for use as a weapon after all.

In any case, we reached the top of the rocky hill without being hit by the "death ray" and stumbled down the other side to my jeep.

Beth still looked dazed as I thrust her inside before hopping behind the wheel.

The tires kicked up a cloud of gravel and dust as I skidded the jeep around in reverse, and then slammed it into drive. Glancing in the rearview mirror, I saw a faint glow, apparently coming from the hidden arroyo, illuminating the top of the hill. It was the same type of glow that had accompanied the saucer's materialization.

"What happened?" Beth asked, craning her neck to look out the back window.

"We had to bug out. Your friends were getting a little too friendly."

She rubbed her blonde head. "I . . . I don't remember."

"I'm not surprised. You were pretty out of it."

"Did the ship leave?"

"I don't think so," I said. "Unless it went after we left. And I don't think it was a ship anyway—it was more like a doorway."

Beth seemed suddenly wide awake once again. "Of course!" she blurted. "That makes perfect sense. That's why the aliens are attracted to the ley lines. They're not from outer space; they're from *hyperspace*—another dimension. The magnetic anomalies must weaken the fabric of space-time separating their dimension from ours. When conditions are right, they can form a portal, step through, and explore."

"Or take samples," I said, looking meaningfully at her.

She blinked, as if trying to clear her head again. "You think they were going to take *me*?" she asked.

"It sure looked like it."

"But why?"

"To study you, maybe. Isn't that what a lot of you UFO people think?"

"I never really believed in alien abduction," she admitted. "I thought it was all psycho-sexual projection."

"Maybe," I said. "Or maybe Mars needs women." I smiled slightly as the jeep bounced over the terrain. Already, the terror of the encounter was slipping away like a bad dream.

"They're *not* from Mars," she scolded, only half serious. "Thanks for getting me out of there. I don't know what came over me. I can only remember bits and pieces."

"Maybe that's what the device the middle guy had was for—like the memory-wipe gizmo Tommy Lee Jones carried in M.I.B."

We reached the highway, and I turned the jeep back toward the hotel, going as fast as the straight, flat road and darkness allowed. I felt more than a bit relieved that we hadn't been disintegrated.

"Maybe it was some kind of a brain scan," Beth suggested. "Maybe the amnesia is just a side effect."

"Could be."

"Do you think they'll come after us?"

"God, I hope not."

"I mean, after all, we saw them, and they didn't get a chance to tamper with *your* memory. And I still remember them, too. Mostly."

That brought back the same bone-chilling feeling I'd had when we first saw the aliens. "Let's hope that they'd rather stay hidden than chase us across the desert and risk being seen," I said. "Do you have a cell phone?"

"Why?"

"To call for help."

"The cops won't believe us."

"So we'll lie to get 'em out here," I said. "Tell them someone's chasing us—that's almost true, anyway. There's safety in numbers, you know."

"I left my cell in my hotel room. I was afraid it might disturb the ley lines. Don't *you* have one?"

"Buried in my luggage," I said. "I like my privacy between assignments."

"So we're screwed." She slumped in the seat and bit her lip in a way that I found very alluring.

"Not yet," I said, still hoping beyond hope that the alternate meaning of the expression might win out before the evening was done.

The highway stretched straight ahead, unspooling before us in headlight-sized puddles. I knew I was overdriving my lights, but I didn't care. I hoped I'd feel safer once we reached the motel, though at the moment, the temptation to drive on past and just keep going was running strong. I cursed myself for not turning northwest; Corona was much closer to us than Roswell, though not as close as the motel. I definitely would have felt more comfortable in a town full of people than in a deserted motel. Unfortunately, most of my gear remained in the Desert View.

In the distance, a soft glow lit the roadway. Before I had time to register it, space folded and the alien saucer appeared ahead of us.

I barely managed to swerve around it. "Son of a bitch!"

The jeep skidded off the road, kicking up a huge cloud of dust. I cut the wheel hard and regained the highway on the other side of the saucer.

Beth stared out the back window, fear etched on her pretty face. "Did you see that?" she gasped. "I've never seen anything move so fast!"

"It didn't move, it emerged, just like before."

"I . . . I don't remember."

"I'm not surprised." Glancing in the rearview mirror, I saw the iris opening in the saucer's surface.

"Hold on to your hat," I told her, pushing the gas pedal all the way to the floor.

As the aliens stepped through the opening, we were moving fast, but not faster than their green lasers.

I felt the rear tires blow even before I smelled the burning rubber and scorched paint. The back windshield shattered, and Beth screamed.

I kept going, fighting the jeep for control. I knew that driving on flat tires would wreck the wheels and probably more, but, at that moment, escaping the aliens was a much higher priority than the health and welfare of my vehicle.

"I thought you said they needed the conjunction of the ley lines!" I snapped. "I thought you said that's how they warped into our dimension!"

"No," she replied, pale with fear. "I said they were attracted to them. But I thought they were coming from outer space . . . I don't know. Maybe once a rift opens, they can travel down the ley lines or something."

"Tell me those lines don't follow this road all the way back to our motel."

"I . . . I don't know. The lines are in flux. That's why I came here. Remember?"

Despite our diminished speed, the saucer and aliens had already vanished into the night behind us. This time, not seeing them didn't lessen our fear. As the jeep rattled on, both of us kept glancing out the back, waiting for the saucer or its strange occupants to appear again.

Stephen D. Sullivan

About a half mile from the hotel, something went "SNAP!" and the jeep ground swiftly to a halt.

"What's wrong?" Beth asked.

I shook my head. "Axle, maybe. Maybe something else."

"Was it their ray gun?"

"Maybe. It could have been all that bouncing around we did in the desert, too—or both. I'm sure as hell not sticking around to find out."

"But where will we go?"

"Back to the motel to call for help. Come on."

I leapt out of the broken jeep, pausing only long enough to grab my camera bag. She got out, too, and we ran as fast as we could to the Desert View Motel.

I found my keys first and let her into the room ahead of me. As she ducked inside, I peered down the highway back the way we'd come, but I didn't see anything—no sign of the aliens or their saucer.

Unfortunately, there was no sign of life in the motel, either; the manager was still out, so we couldn't expect any help from that quarter.

"The phone's dead," Beth announced.

I swore, shut the door, and fished my cell out of my luggage. "No signal. Crap!" The in-room phone wasn't working, either.

"Do you think they've done something? Maybe their weapons affect the phones somehow?"

"Like in that old Martian invasion movie?" I asked. "I guess that's possible. Either way, it's our tough luck."

She moved to turn on the light.

"Don't!" I barked. "It'll just attract their attention—if they're out there."

She went to the window and peeked through the crack between the heavy curtains.

"See anything?"

"No."

"How long will the conjunction of those ley lines last?" I asked.

"Just tonight . . . I think."

"So if we hold out until morning, we should be safe."

"M-maybe."

"I never travel armed. Do you have any weapons in your room?"

She shook her head. "N-no. But I still have that beer."

"You better get it, then." I said. "I'll see if I can find something in the manager's office. A secluded place like this might have a weapon handy, just in case."

"I'll meet you back here."

"Right." Both of us ducked out the door, making sure the coast was clear both ways before we left. I went to the office, while she hurried back to her own room.

It took me the better part of ten minutes to break open the door, jimmy the office desk, and find the sawed-off shotgun hidden inside. I figured I could apologize to the management later—*if* we made it through the night.

When I finally returned to my room, Beth had a flashlight as well as the beer. She also had my camera out and had discovered the small photo printer I keep in the camera bag. As I closed the door behind me, she was busy printing out several of the shots I'd taken during our frightening encounter.

"These are the best alien photos I've ever seen," she gushed.

I appraised them with my photographer's eye. They were badly framed and more out of focus than I would have liked.

"They suck," I said. Then I smiled. "But they still might be good enough for a Pulitzer."

"What do we do now?"

I checked to make sure the shotgun's safety was off. "Now we hole up here and wait. If we last until sunrise, maybe we'll live long enough to collect that prize. Hand me one of those beers, would you?"

She did, kissing me as she handed it over. "Thanks," she breathed. "For everything."

I smiled and kissed her back.

Lindarino --

I hacked this inter-company email from *The National Traveler* assignment editor, Shelly Greenberg's account.

The note is addressed to *TNT* Editor In Chief Arthur Edwards, but I couldn't find the original email alluded to or any follow-up. Nor could I hack their voicemail system.

I'll keep trying, though.

Do you think Beth might have been right about that Roswell stuff?

-- Chuck
PSI-ET co-chair, Frosthaven, WI.

Arthur,

Despite the cryptic message on my voicemail, I don't know who Beth Rhule is or what connection she may have to Tom going missing. The Corona (NM) authorities tell me she's a bank receptionist from Wisconsin with ties to a fringe paranormal group <Ha! - Chuck> known as PSI-ET. They believe his disappearance may have something to do with the occult, <Again - Ha!> based on the remains of several cleverly-faked photographs found at the scene. <Wonder what *those* were?>

So far as I know, Tom has never had any connection with that or any other fringe group; he's always been very reliable.

Police have thoroughly searched the scorched ruins of the Desert View Motel, where Henderson and Rhule were staying, and found no trace of either of them in the ashes.

The cause of the blaze that destroyed the motel remains undetermined. The local papers have been playing up the freak meteor hit theory, but the cops aren't buying that. If the authorities have any clue as to the whereabouts of Tom or the girl, they're not saying.

I'm hoping that maybe the two of them have just run off to Vegas or something; you know Tom can be a bit of a wolf.

I realize we need that Carlsbad Caverns piece ASAP, so I've sent another photographer to re-shoot Tom's work. It's surprising Tom didn't download the lot to our servers after finishing the assignment, though he did mention lack of internet when he called from the ill-fated motel. \<Rats! - Chuck\> He was hoping to find an internet café and send the photos in the morning, but obviously he never got the chance.

In hopes of salvaging this assignment before deadline, I asked another freelancer in the area to drive out to Corona and try to track Tom down. If we can turn him up, maybe we can still make the October issue.

Unfortunately, I haven't heard back from that reporter in the last few days, either.

Why is good help so hard to find?
Concerned,
Shelly

VANDALS... Part II
by Robert E Vardeman

"Anomaly along space-time vector 2!"

The saucer-shaped craft began wobbling, throwing the two occupants around. Mornn ran his tendrils over the controls and sensed the energy flow through the glowing crystals with a skill unmatched in any of the cross-dimensional realms. He closed his large eyes and became one with the zeta energy flow that controlled their vessel. The good ship *Plunderer* responded immediately. The small bubble in the dark energy ocean had amounted to nothing, but crossing ten spacial dimensions and two of time required constant vigilance. Mornn had lost three creche mates and a good friend because they had not heeded his warning about venturing onto this particular frontier world. Only vigilance would ensure a safe visit.

"We should never have attempted this," Peggl complained. He stretched out his spindly arms to an impossible width to adjust the engines. "It's illegal to scavenge on this world for a reason."

"The reason is that the Consortium wants all the profits for itself. Who is the Ruling One to put this planet off limits to archeologists?"

"Archeologists?" Peggl added several expletives to his thought pattern to show his disdain for such subterfuge. "Is that what we call ourselves when the Enforcers catch us?"

"They won't catch us," Mornn insisted. He played the control panel like a well-tuned musical instrument, listening to the energies sing and watching them dance to the tune he knew would rise from his every touch, no matter how fleeting. "This world is too primitive to place on a Do Not Exploit list."

"Too primitive? Isn't that the reason it was put there so we wouldn't try to steal from them or sell them a second sun or something equally illegal?"

"The word is that the planet was put on the list because of a crude fission weapon detonation."

"Really?" This caught Peggl's attention. "I am interested in artificial glasses made from intense radiation."

"They call it trinitite on this world, and I've located acres of it." Mornn sensed his friend's interest. They all had their personal enthusiasms, those who dared sneak about the continuum, ignoring the warnings put out by the bureaucrats. It wasn't as if they were going to exploit the world—really *exploit* it—like the Consortium would. He had seen entire worlds encased in carbon so the interior could be hollowed out for myriad industries. That was exploitation. Those worlds glowed red-hot all the time, ridding themselves of the waste heat generated under the surface. Or the Consortium mined iceteroids and planetesimals until there was nothing left in a solar system but debris. That was exploitation. What he and Peggl intended was more like . . . collecting souvenirs.

This primitive world had few enough aircraft and nothing reaching into space, though he had watched one puny little rocket shoot up almost twenty miles. Fireworks set off by creche officials to celebrate new hatchling arrivals produced more bang than the silly little package that had parachuted back to the ground. It had been moderately amusing, but also depressing, watching the lumbering giants rush to find their equipment. They were so big and clumsy.

Peggl might scoop up a ton or two of the green radioactive glass but Mornn wanted more. The natives roared about in smelly four-wheeled vehicles powered by organic fuels. One or two of those posted for sale on GalBuy ought to get bids from serious collectors all over the galaxy and possibly from some of the outposts in time. He had studied a guide on how best to post biddable items and how to obtain the best money for them. A car, as the natives called their vehicles, would fetch enough for him to retire. Who else dared sneak past the Enforcers to snag one of the noisome machines? If he got enough fuel to power it for a year or two, he could not only retire but do so on a pleasure planet.

He had heard of one three dimensions over and one time-dimension down that catered to adventurers like him and Peggl.

"We're going to get caught. I know it, Mornn."

He hid the thought behind his mind block: *adventurers like me.*

"What's that?"

"Nothing. I wanted a scan of the terrain for alpha and beta radioactivity."

"For the trinitite, yes," Peggl responded eagerly. He worked for a few seconds, then asked, "Why do you call it trinitite? How do you know the native name?"

Mornn worked to keep his shield up to hide that he had twice been to this world—without his partner. The two adventures had whetted his appetite for further exploration. The natives, who called themselves man or possibly woman—it was confusing how their terminology changed—were clever for primitives. Their machines were cunningly constructed and a cuckoo clock he had taken back on his last visit had fetched a fine price on the curio black market. He had almost kept the falling weight powered time device for himself, but he spent too much of his life in the *Plunderer* and the shifting graviton field to expect it to keep time equal to the celestial wave clock used by his vessel.

Still, it had a nice look and feel to it. Mornn rippled his tendrils in memory.

"They tested at a site they called Trinity, not far away."

"Radioactive glass? You are certain?"

"All you want," Mornn assured his friend, "but I have to find my vehicle first. There are several around here."

"Why not go to the fission bomb test area and look for vehicles there?"

Mornn didn't want to explain the idea of armed guards. When he had brought the *Plunderer* in low on a solo run a few local weeks earlier, he had been shot at. The puny weapons did nothing, but one larger weapon had dented the hull. It had been an accidental hit because of the nature of their weapons and the sophisticated defenses his ship used, but Mornn was reluctant to discuss all that had might go wrong if they went directly to the test site to hunt for vehicles—and Peggl's precious radioactive green glass.

"They are easier to find here," Mornn lied. He fought to keep his block up to prevent his friend from seeing the details of the earlier exploration. They had agreed to never pillage in this dimensional world alone because of the danger, but Mornn had wanted some spoils all for himself. Arranging the dual time dimension so he returned an instant after he left had been difficult, but it had also been profitable.

He had loaded the *Plunderer* with the contents of an entire roadside attraction called Desert Bob's Reptile Ranch. Whatever mystery the mans of this world saw there perplexed him, but the trinkets had sold well on GalBuy and would finance a fine vacation later. Why divvy the take with even an old friend as helpful as Peggl? After all, Peggl could collect all the green fused silicate matter he wanted and keep the proceeds when he sold it.

"Is that one of your vehicles below? It is unmoving."

Mornn quickly touched the nearest shining white gem controller embedded in the control panel, adjusting its hue to a dull red glow. As he did, the scene below entered his brain directly and allowed him to scan the entire region.

"It is, and there are no mans around. It is abandoned. Perfect!"

"What if it is damaged? We won't get as much for it then, will we?"

Mornn shielded his disgust at the way Peggl counted himself into the vehicular contraband. Mornn wasn't asking to share the trinitite. Why should Peggl want any part of the sale of the vehicle?

"You are distressed. I sense it leaking from behind your privacy block," Peggl said. "We are partners."

"Even if the Enforcers catch us?"

Mornn was not surprised that answering took Peggl several seconds.

"You are the crook. I am the unwilling dupe."

"So far. Until we load the radioactive glass. If the Enforcers need something to track, that will be what they detect first. There are no ID markers on the vehicles."

"That makes them safer, but also more dangerous if we are caught since they will obviously be stolen primitive machines."

Mornn was in no mood to debate the point. He guided the *Plunderer* to a spot near the unmoving man vehicle and brought the ship down slowly until it hovered an easy step down. With practiced ease, he secured the control panel.

"Join me in examining the vehicle?"

"It is oxidized," Peggl said, stroking his controllers, "and will not function."

"It is a derelict?" Mornn hid a flash of irritation. He wanted a working artifact from this world since it was embargoed but might be opened for tourism at any time. When the cruise lines began routine excursions, no one would want to buy an artifact because they could get them on their own trip. Some tourists even thought a picture of a native in its natural environment was superior to possessing the native artifacts themselves.

"We can examine it," Peggl said. "My study of the device might be faulty. I am used to hyper-dimensional drives, not ridiculous organic-fuel-burning engines."

Mornn flicked a tendril over a control, causing the green light to fade to a dull purple. The cargo hatch in the center of the disk opened for them to leave the control room.

Heads almost touching, the two friends mentally exchanged scenarios of what they would find and how best to recover and store the vehicle for transport home. They walked briskly into empty space and were gently lowered to the ground, never breaking stride. The immensity within the vessel belied the compact exterior. The energy required to move hyper-dimensionally depended on exterior surface area, not volume, so Mornn kept the *Plunderer* as small as possible outside and as large inside as feasible.

They stepped out from under the silvery hull and paused a moment.

"Suns," said Peggl, looking up into the night. "What happened to them in the sky?"

"This planet is out on one arm of the galaxy. This is all they see at night."

"How sad. Everything about this world is lacking."

"Except the trinitite," Mornn reminded him.

They strode away, their pace slow and their legs bowing slightly under the heavy gravity until they found the vehicle half buried in the desert sand. Mornn kicked at it and saw Peggl had analyzed accurately. The rusted hull would never bring a decent price, even on relic-starved worlds.

"We must find another vehicle. This will not do," Mornn said, not trying to disguise his vexation.

"The radioactive glass field in only a few seconds flight over the mountains. We can find you a suitable vehicle there."

"Car," Mornn said. "The mans call them cars."

Peggl stopped and inclined his head toward Mornn's, sending out a stronger telepathic signal. Both stared at the *Plunderer* and the native crouched below the open cargo hatch.

"Does he see us?"

"I don't know," answered Mornn. "He isn't telepathic." He jumped when the human screeched and ran up the hill, kicking up a cloud of sand behind him as he went.

"We are lucky that was only an inhabitant. If an Enforcer had found us ..."

"You worry too much," Mornn said. They positioned themselves at the point where the force beam lifted them into the ship. Mornn gestured, closed the hatch and then went to control panel.

"NO!"

Peggl screeched in pain at his friend's intense telepathic outburst.

"Shield yourself," Peggl said in distress. "You burned out all my neurons."

"He crippled the ship. He took the control crystals!"

Peggl noticed that the internal gravity field matched that of the world as he shuffled to his position at the controls. His own anguish merged with his friend's as he realized how completely they had been sabotaged.

"The dimensional drive is disabled," Peggl said.

"The man stole the stabilization controllers, too. We can launch but will wobble. And there is no way we can return home. All of the time dimension 2 controllers are missing."

"We do not have spares," Peggl pointed out needlessly. The desolate telepathic communication from Mornn told of his understanding. They were stranded on this primitive world unless they recovered the stolen equipment.

"Lifting off," Mornn said. "We must find the man immediately. Otherwise, he will go away in a vehicle and disappear."

"How do you know he came in a vehicle?"

"Their legs are incapable of functioning long in this heavy gravity. You walk slowly. They must, also, and need the vehicles to get about."

The *Plunderer* rose, shook all over and caused more problems to light up the control panel. Mornn took in the warning messages changing color and meaning. Being discovered by the Enforcers might be a mercy. At least they could spend the rest of their lives on a prison world rather than trapped on this backward planet.

"I detect a vehicle," Peggl said. "With one man. There is another standing nearby."

Mornn absorbed the telepathic directions and maneuvered the vessel to the best of his ability. It was buffeted about by graviton waves, but he kept from crashing as he followed the fleeing vehicle. It kicked up a dust cloud, making pursuit easy, but the *Plunderer* became increasingly erratic because of the missing controller crystals.

"What of the second man?"

"One at a time," Mornn said grimly. "I no longer have the power to bring the entire vehicle into the cargo hold, but I can use the force beams on the native." Even as he communicated with Peggl, he worked. Enough control remained for him to open the hatch, then focus the energy beam and lift the man. A final pass with his tendril closed the hatch and dropped the screaming, fighting man to the deck.

"We can appeal to his good nature to return what he has stolen," Mornn said. He and Peggl walked toward the man. He reached out a hand in what he had seen as some sort of peaceful greeting. The natives gripped one another's appendages and moved them about in a ritualistic fashion.

"He is frightened and avoids your greeting of man friendship," Peggl said.

Mornn let out a psychic roar of pain as the native rushed forward and grabbed his arm, twisting viciously. Mornn regained control of his nervous system and deleted the appendage, letting the man yank it away. Mornn and Peggl retreated to a spot near the sabotaged control panel and put their heads close to enhance communication.

"It is a wild beast," Peggl said. "We must evict it immediately!"

"It must know where the controllers are. Without them, we are stranded on this world."

"I agree that this thing knows where they are. How do we persuade it to return what it has taken? Force?"

"We can negotiate with it. While it lacks telepathic power, it is equipped with an information jack such as used by the Gorkannians and others lacking transfrontal lobes."

"Yes, you are right," Peggl said. "Do you think it is agreeing to our communication attempt by waving around your discarded appendage?"

Mornn was no longer sure what to make of the native. He had to assume some rational behavior existed within and that, once the communications pod was installed, a flow of information would be possible. He reached his remaining limb out, found the proper control and altered the color slightly. The man let out a cry of agreement as the force beam floated him to the communications console.

"I am prepared to attach the grounding straps," Peggl said.

"Do so. I will strip off the protective layer and insert the communications pod."

Using the force beam he lofted the slender silver cylinder, guided it to the data port and inserted.

"Something is wrong!" Peggl became frantic at the man's wild behavior.

"Interfacing," Mornn said, ignoring the thrashing about. The four grounding straps were in place, as was the com pod. He began adjusting his equipment but was unable to locate the proper frequency to lock in meaningful communication.

"The native is too primitive for civilized communication. No telepathy, no workable data port." Peggl shook his head in disgust, but Mornn refused to give up so easily. He increased the voltage, hoping this would establish a better connection. The man collapsed on the table and all but the carrier brain wave ceased.

"You are right," Mornn said. "It leaks noxious fluids, since there seems no control over this expulsion. The com pod is not responding with any wave pattern I can decipher." He increased the voltage a little more, hoping this would find the proper resonance with the creature, but only spasmodic twitches rewarded the effort.

"I have found the controllers! They were hidden in the outer synthetic skin!"

Mornn saw Peggl holding the missing controllers. He radiated approval and appreciation for his friend, then concentrated on growing a new appendage. Both hands would be required to recalibrate the crystals and get the *Plunderer* into dimension-hopping trim.

"Are all the crystals properly socketed?" asked Mornn.

"I am running new checks, but so far there is not a malfunction. The crystals were not damaged."

"If he had cracked even one of them, we might never regain full power for the dimensional drive," Mornn said. He worked diligently to align the potent flows of dark energy through the wave guides that built power in the engines. As he glided from one side of the control panel to the other, reaching here and adjusting there, he began a scan of the surrounding area below. If the *Plunderer* once more functioned, there was no reason to abandon their quest for vehicles and radioactive glass. After all they had endured on this worthless water-ball of a planet, they deserved to make a huge take off the run.

"I have found the vehicle the native used," Mornn said. "It has been wrecked. However, I have found another one nearby, heavier and more powerful." His mind worked over the possibilities of an even bigger vehicle going for auction. So many beings in the Consortium really thought bigger was better. Mornn would gladly trade these fuming, noisy behemoths for a single wheeler any day.

There was no accounting for the tastes of collectors—or those who supplied the items they desired most.

"Power levels remain low," Peggl said. "One of the controllers taken kept the temporal capacitance at a maximum. Without it, we lost power."

"We bled off most of our stored temporalitrons when the field was removed," Mornn agreed. "We are rebuilding reserves at optimal speed."

"Can we depart for home, if we are not at full reserve?"

"What is wrong?" Mornn caught Peggl's uneasiness. "We have all the time we need to get your glass and my vehicle. I have one located almost directly below us."

"The distant warning system was disabled, but I transferred power from lesser systems," Peggl said. "Can you make out the approaching craft?"

Mornn turned frantic, his tendrils slipping and sliding in a wild glissando when he caught the hailing signal from the other ship.

"Enforcers!"

"You said they'd never find us. What will we do?"

"Quiet," Mornn said, working faster now. "We have restored enough power to get away. All we need are a few minutes to build speed for a cross-dimensional transition."

"Can we do that in this thick fog they call an atmosphere?"

"We have no choice." Mornn froze when control lights changed subtly. He spun and saw the man banging on the deck in an effort to open the cargo hatch. Reaching back, Mornn touched the proper switch. The hatch opened and the man dropped from sight.

"That is good. He cannot testify against us when the Enforcers bring us to trial," Peggl groaned.

"How would they get testimony from him? He was a mute." Mornn swung back and worked faster on his control panel. The *Plunderer* was a good ship, one equipped with stealth devices to elude the Enforcers, but Mornn had to choose between speed and furtiveness. They had not restored enough power for both.

"Prepare for dimensional shift."

"Space-time vector 2 aligned," Peggl confirmed.

"Let's not get caught." Mornn swung the vessel about in a hook trajectory. He got one last look at the vehicle below, moving along slowly at the front of a dust cloud kicked up by its four ground-based wheels. He felt a pang of regret. He could have been rich if he had snared such an artifact.

Peggl could have been rich if they had scooped up the trinitite before pursuing the vehicle.

Mornn regretted everything about his experiences on this backward planet.

"I'll get me something better than a vehicle next time," he vowed. "And I'll find a native who can communicate through his data port. This one must have been defective."

Then all thought of the future was wiped away as he concentrated completely on building speed and sliding the *Plunderer* through twelve dimensions to avoid the pursuing Enforcer vessel.

Two brilliant green trails scarred the Earth's night sky—and then both ships shifted dimensions and vanished completely.

ABOUT THE CONTRIBUTORS

JIM HOLLOWAY — Cover Artist

Jim Holloway doesn't consider himself worth talking about, despite more than twenty-five years as a professional artist working on everything from D&D to Paranoia to the RPGA to Endless Quest books. His illustration of the craft is based on his own research into what happened at Roswell. Look for more of Jim's work in future Walkabout Publishing products, and at better book and game stores everywhere.

JEAN E. RABE – "Eighteen"

Jean Rabe is the author of more than two dozen novels and four dozen stories. She believes in aliens, enjoys tugging on old socks with her dogs, and plays in multiple fantasy football leagues (and occasionally wins). She maintains a website she likes folks to visit: www.jeanrabe.com.

NICK REDFERN – "Roswell, Parts I & II"

Nick Redfern is the author of many books on UFOs, cryptozoology and the paranormal, including *There's Something in the Woods*, *Strange Secrets*, *Three Men Seeking Monsters*, *The FBI Files*, *A Covert Agenda*, *On the Trail of the Saucer Spies*, and *Man-Monkey*. Nick writes regularly for *UFO Magazine*, Britain's *Paranormal*, and *Fate*. He can be contacted at his website: www.nickredfern.com.

STEPHEN D. SULLIVAN – "Last Call at Corona"

Steve Sullivan has been interested in flying saucers since one flew past the alcove window of his house in Morristown, New Jersey during the early 1960s. Since then, he has written numerous fantasy, Sci-Fi, and horror stories, novels, and comic books, worked on countless popular role-playing and board games, and become the host of a weekly radio program, *Uncanny Radio*— www.uncannyworld.com. You can find a sampling of his stories in *Martian Knights & Other Tales* and *Zombies, Werewolves, & Unicorns*. Steve continues to be interested in all things strange and paranormal. Contact him through his website: www.stephendsullivan.com.

ROBERT E. VARDEMAN – "Vandals... Parts I & II"

Born in the year of the Roswell crash, Robert E Vardeman is the author of more than a hundred novels and sixty short stories (many collected in *Stories from Desert Bob's Reptile Ranch*). His most recent science fiction novel is *Moonlight in the Meg*, available as an e-book app from the iTunes store. For more information on this and other fiction, see the author's website: www.cenotaphroad.com.

WALKABOUT PUBLISHING
Great stories by great authors.

Robert E. Vardeman—Marc Tassin—James M. Ward—Nick Redfern
Lorelei Shannon—Dean Leggett—Kathleen Watness—Paul Genesse
E. Readicker-Henderson—Jason Mical——Kelly Swails—Brandie Tarvin
Stephen D. Sullivan—Jean Rabe—And More!

Pirates of the Blue Kingdoms
Blue Kingdoms: Buxom Buccaneers
Blue Kingdoms: Shades & Specters
Blue Kingdoms: Zombies, Werewolves, & Unicorns
Luck o' the Irish
Martian Knights & Other Stories
Stories from Desert Bob's Reptile Ranch
This and That and Tales About Cats
Under the Protection of the Cow Demon

Walkabout Publishing
P.O. Box 151
Kansasville, WI 53139
www.walkaboutpublishing.com

Official Home of Uncanny Encounters.